TUTUS & COWBOY BOOTS

PART ONE

CASEY PEELER

Tutus & Cowboy Boots
A Small Town Dance Romance
Part One

By Casey Peeler

Tutus & Cowboy Boots Part One- 1st Edition
Edited by Beth Suit at BB Books
Cover by Pam Baldwin at Paperclutch
Paperback ISBN: 978-1517614416
Digital ISBN: 9780996152150
Copyright © 2015 Casey Peeler

ALSO BY CASEY PEELER

Boondocks

Crashing Tides

Full Circle Series
(Losing Charley, Finding Charley & Loving Charley)
Full Circle Series Box Set

Lion Eyes

Our Song

Southern Perfection

Tutus & Cowboy Boots Part 2

Worth the Ride

1

CADENCE

I grab my dance bag and toss it over my shoulder. Lauren, my best friend and duet partner, walks out of the dance studio behind me.

"So this is it," she says with sadness in her voice.

"I guess so. What am I going to do without you?" I ask as she embraces me. "I mean why did my dad have to do something so stupid? And why am I the one being punished for it?" I ask as we pull apart.

"Just promise me if you have a chance to come back home, you will. I don't know how you're going to survive out there in the middle of nowhere. Do they even have cellphones?" Lauren questions.

"Yeah, I'm sure they do but who knows if there will be any signal in the middle of a field. Well, I better get going. I have dinner tonight with Dad and his home-wrecking secretary. Maybe if I put on a smile, he'll change his mind."

"I got my fingers crossed," she says while holding up her hands. I smile, but deep down I know better. My father is selfish. Not only did he mess around with his secretary, but he didn't even put up a fight for me so tonight is our goodbye dinner. I know Lauren wants me to come back, but it will never happen. I just hope and pray that my future isn't as bleak as I envision it.

As I walk into our spacious apartment, I quickly drop my dance bag in the laundry room and hurry to get ready. Dad moved out six months ago and now this house is cold and the memories that made it a home are all distorted. I knew Mom would sell it eventually, but I wasn't prepared for her to move out of the city. And we're not just moving to the suburbs, we're moving to Hillbilly, USA. Never in my life did I think my mom would resort back to her Southern roots. She always told me she left for a full-ride to NYU and she'd never move back. When she met my dad, I'm betting she didn't see this in her future. Tomorrow morning, we're loading up our new Suburban, also known as our peace offering from Dad, and heading south to Delight, North Carolina. I can tell you right now, there's nothing delightful about that town.

I check the time on my phone and have exactly fifteen minutes to catch the subway to get to Dad's on time. I arrive at the station with five minutes to spare. As I stand waiting on the platform, I wonder if he's going to do something special tonight. Oh! Maybe he's changed his mind and will ask me to stay. I continue to ponder the possibilities as I take my seat. At exactly seven o'clock I knock on Dad's door and am greeted by the home-wrecking bimbo. I smile as sweetly as possible, but underneath I want to take my nails and mess up that pretty face and rip out that bleach-blond hair. She lets me know Dad is in his office as I step into the apartment.

"Hey Dad," I say as I lean on the doorframe.

"Hey Cadence. How was school and dance today?" he questions like he genuinely cares.

"It was great! I had so much fun telling everyone goodbye," I say sarcastically.

He pauses and looks at me. "Don't be like this. You're leaving tomorrow. Can we please have a pleasant night?"

"Of course," I say as I turn to help the bimbo set the table.

Dinner is the same routine it has been each week since he moved out. I try to convince him to let me stay here and he gives me the same story about needing time with the bimbo, and making their relationship work. I want to scream, *what about our relationship? I'm your favorite girl.* At least that's what he always said. I guess he lied.

When we finish eating, I leave my dishes on the table. That witch can clean them her own self. Dad asks me to sit on the patio with him. He makes small talk for a few minutes, and then I know what's coming. Goodbye.

"Cadence, I really wish things were different, but your mother believes that going to Delight will be best for you. I agree."

"What about what I think? I've lived in New York my entire life. Do you really think that I'm going to be able to fit in, in that speck of a town? Not to mention it's my senior year. I have some amazing companies looking at me. Dad, everything is done. I need to be with Lauren. We've already choreographed our senior piece. How am I going to find a partner, learn a new piece and find a decent school? These are big name companies. They don't want someone from some little hick town. You sent me to these schools because they were the best. Do you honestly think the best are in Delight, North Carolina?"

"It will work out."

"Right, just like you and Mom." I stand. "I guess I need to get home so I can finish packing," I say as I stalk toward the door.

"Cadence, don't do this. I don't want you to leave like this." I start to laugh as I turn to face him.

"Funny thing is. You didn't think once about me and how I felt when you put our family second. Bye Dad." As I open the door, he calls to me.

"Cadence!" I take in a deep breath and stop in the doorway. "No matter what I love you. Just remember that." I nod.

"Love you too, Dad," I say as I close the door. It's true because no matter what, he's my dad.

Walking up to our building, I see every light on in our apartment. I take a deep breath. I don't want to cry. I want to be mad. Mad at my dad who doesn't want me and mad at my mom who is taking me away from everything I've ever known. I check my reflection in my camera app to make sure no tears have escaped and then make my way inside.

"Cade, is that you?" Mom asks as I pass her bedroom.

"Yes," I say hurrying to my room. I don't want to talk right now.

"How did it go?"

I laugh. "How do you think?"

I kick off my shoes, and Mom walks into my room as I begin to remove my jewelry. "That bad, huh?"

"Oh, best time ever, Mom," I scoff.

"I'm sorry," she says as she pulls me into her arms. I refuse to cry in front of her.

"It's okay. I don't need him."

"Actually, it's not. As much as I want to say you don't need him. I know that he's your dad, and you do. Things will change. Just give it time." I nod. "Now, you need to go to bed soon. Tomorrow is going to be a long day. The movers will be here at eight."

"Okay. Night Mom," I say.

"Love you, Cadence."

"Love you, too."

2

CADENCE

"*C*adence." I hear my mom's voice as she knocks on the door. I pull the covers over my head. "Cade. It's time to get up," she says. I hear my door creak open and know I have no choice. It's time to face reality. My life, as I know it, is over. Feeling a dip in the bed, I wait to hear what she has to say next.

"Honey, I hate this as much as you do, but it's what's best for us. Gran is willing to let us stay with her until we can get on our feet. Who knows maybe you'll even like it there," she says as she pulls the covers back. I pull my pillow on top of my head to keep out the light. "Seriously, Cadence. We don't have much time. The moving crew will be here soon." Knowing there are only a few items left to move, I get out of bed. "That's my girl. Come on. Once they finish up, we'll be on our way."

I put on something fashionable yet comfortable for our ten-hour ride to Delight. Pulling the covers off my bed, I quickly fold the comforter and say goodbye to my bed. I might have to say goodbye to it, but there's no way I'm leaving my Lilly Pulitzer comforter. That's out!

Walking toward the foyer, Mom stares at me. "What?" I ask.

"You know we can buy a new one," she says.

"Yeah, but this is mine, and I'm not leaving it," I say.

She shrugs her shoulders, and brushes it off. We take the remainder of our personal items and place them in the Suburban. Thankfully, Mom has shipped most of our clothes and valuables. We are taking a final look around the apartment when the movers arrive. Not only is Mom selling the apartment, she's selling all the furniture. She said Gran has everything we need for now so it's not worth taking it with us. Gran's idea of décor and this place are polar opposites so I think Mom is crazy for not wanting to keep our stuff. When I pushed her to keep some of it, she grumbled something about not wanting any of *his* crap as a reminder. It all just sucks and Gran's house is a time warp to the sixties with god-awful country flair. It would be nice to have some pieces to remind me of home.

After the trucks are packed with the rest of our stuff, we decide to stop by my favorite bakery for a flavored coffee and freshly baked croissant for breakfast. As Mom drives out of the city, I quietly eat my breakfast and we make small talk. After we merge onto the interstate, she cranks up the radio and sets the cruise control. I text Lauren until she has to leave for the studio, and wish I was going with her.

BARRICK

I roll out of bed before the rooster crows, slide on my worn out jeans and shirt, and then grab my boots and head toward the kitchen. Setting my boots by my chair, I open the refrigerator and grab the orange juice and drink straight from the carton.

"Barrick! You know better," Mama says as she hands me a glass.

"Sorry, but it tastes better this way," I admit.

"You sure it doesn't have to do with not wanting to do the dishes?"

I shrug my shoulders. "What time you think you'll be home tonight?" she asks as she twists her hair into a funky knot on the top of her head.

"Probably four. Ms. Brown said she wanted to stop a little early today."

"Are you serious? That doesn't sound like her," Mama says.

"Yeah she's got family comin' into town." Mama doesn't say anything, but I can tell by her stance that she's thinking about something. I finish my juice and slide on my boots. I slide my worn out ball cap on my head, pick up my truck keys, and grab a fried apple pie on the way out the door.

Arriving at the Brown's farm, I pull my truck alongside the barn and notice the lights are on. Walking inside, I see Ms. Brown filling the feed buckets for the horses.

"Mornin' Ms. Brown," I say.

She stops and turns to me. "Boy, I've told you to quit calling me that! It's Mae Ellen or Mae, but not Ms. Brown. Now, grab that feed and get moving. We got a lot to do today, and not a lot of time."

"Yes Ms. Mae," I say.

"That's better," she says as she continues to work.

I spend most of the morning with the dairy cows. I swear I've seen more cow milk in the past two months than in my entire life. Who would have thought that a farm in little old Delight could be such an asset to our county and the foothills of North Carolina? When Mr. Brown passed away three years ago, my older brother, Bo, helped Ms. Mae. Now that he is overseas with the Marines, she asked if I'd like to help. I had no idea what this job actually entailed.

After lunch Ms. Mae asks me to do a few things out of the ordinary. This woman's got me carrying boxes, mopping, and even wants me to go to the grocery store for her. The only time she's ever asked me for help inside was to fix a broken door handle. I don't ask any questions, I say "Yes ma'am" as she gives me each task. She must really be excited about her family coming to town.

As I set the groceries on the table, I hear her holler for me to come help her upstairs. When I make my way into the room, I hurry a little bit more when I realize she's struggling to move a dresser. I quickly grab the other side, and we both move it with ease.

"'nything else Ms. Mae?" I question.

"Nah, I've just got to make the beds and I think I'm about finished. You've been such a big help 'round here. Thank you."

"No problem," I say as I help her neatly stack boxes in the corner of the room.

Glancing at her watch, she informs me it's a little after three. "Go ahead and call it an early day Barrick. I'm going to finish up here and then relax a little bit."

"You sure?" I question.

"Yeah, just be here at normal time tomorrow."

CADENCE

Staring out the passenger side window, I can't help but wish my life were different. The farther down the interstate we drive, the faster my dreams fade behind me. Who knew that one act—or maybe more—by my father would impact my life to this extent? I cannot stand him.

Hearing my phone beep, I take my phone from my purse. Touching the screen, I see a picture from Lauren. It's a selfie of her in the studio with a pouty face. I smile knowing that she's missing me, but seeing the studio makes tears well up in my eyes. I quickly wipe them away, grab my ear buds and turn on my favorite playlist.

Mom and I make fairly good time, but I'm so tired of being in this vehicle. We stop every few hours to stretch, use the restroom, and get a snack. When we hit the North Carolina state line I get excited, but my excitement is quickly extinguished when I realize we still have a few more hours to go.

As the sun begins to set, the light is blinding as we drive west on Interstate 40, but once it's behind the trees we're no longer squinting behind our sunglasses. We make a turn off the interstate and Mom calls Gran to let her know we're almost there. She says that she has dinner waiting for us, and I can only imagine what varmint she's fried up.

As if she's reading my mind, Mom looks at me. "Stop it. You know she's not going to feed you something crazy."

"You never know, but I bet no matter what it's something fried and a million carbs," I say with attitude, and Mom pulls the car off to the side.

"Look, I left Delight thinking I'd never go back, but sometimes we can't control what happens in our lives. I know that this isn't want you want to do right now, but I didn't want a divorce either. As much as you think your life is over, it's not. Take a moment and think about me Cadence. I've lost everything I've worked for *and* your father. The least you can do is be grateful that Gran is letting us move in with her. Now I'd appreciate you putting a smile on your face when we get to Gran's just like I'm going to do."

I don't say anything because if I did she'd probably make me walk the rest of the way to Gran's and there's no way I'm walking out here by myself.

Mom drives in silence as I stare out the window. We finally arrive in Delight, and when I say we've arrived I mean we've passed a tiny green rectangular sign with the word Delight on it. There's no post office, shops or anything. It's a speck of a community near an extremely small town called Lawndale where there isn't a chain restaurant for thirty miles.

Turning onto the gravel driveway I see the glow of the lights in the farmhouse. Once Mom puts the Suburban in park, I open the door and almost vomit from the stench that invades my nose.

"What is that smell?" I ask as I hold my nose.

She starts to laugh. "Cadence, it's the country, but more than likely that's a bunch of cow manure."

Oh. My. Gosh. I woke up in New York and landed in hades. I quickly grab my essentials and as I begin to walk toward the house, I trip over something. I squeal and catch my balance. "Why's it so dark out here?"

"Cadence, honey, this is the way God made it. There aren't any street lamps. Just give your eyes a moment to adjust." I do and it helps, but before I take another step, I grab my phone and turn on my flashlight. I then drop my essentials on the ground.

"No service! Mom! My phone has no service!"

"You'll survive. Gran has a landline." Who is this lady and where did my mother go? Shoot me now!

CADENCE

*W*alking into Gran's house is like walking into a wildlife exhibit at the zoo. There are animals everywhere but not one of them is alive. They are all stuffed. It is so gross; it's like they are staring at me. I drop my bags on the staircase, and Gran greets me with her hands on her hips.

"Excuse me young lady, but that is not where those belong." I expel a huge breath and roll my eyes as I pick up my things.

"Then where do I take them?" I sass back.

Gran looks at Mom. "Who is this? This is not my sweet Cadence."

"Mom…" my mom says, but Gran cuts in.

"I know for a fact I didn't bring you up like this, and you better pray to the big man upstairs that this one right here changes her tune quick."

"Cadence, take your stuff to your room right now, and drop the attitude," Mom says. I'm disgusted that my mom, who always stood up to my dad and had been a strong person, does what Gran says without question. She's a grown-ass adult.

"Well, which room would that be?" I ask with my hand on my hip.

"Top of the steps and third door on the right," Gran instructs while mimicking me with her hand on her hip.

Without another word, I clomp up the steps to make my grand exit. Looking at the top of the stairs I see a picture of Gramps, Gran, and Mom when she was in high school. I almost laugh. She looks nothing like she does today. She has braided hair and is wearing overalls. Did I mention she was in *high school*? Glancing over my shoulder I see a polished editor in designer clothes sporting a trendy hairstyle. She's gorgeous.

Standing outside my new room, I hold my breath as I push open the door. Oh my gosh, everything is baby food pea green. The wallpaper is older than me, and what is that smell? I drop my items on the comforter that looks like a rug and walk toward the dresser, where I see a mixture of dried flowers and wooden chips in a bowl on top of the dresser. I pick up a piece and cautiously sniff it. It smells like pine trees and cinnamon. Ew, they have got to go! I empty the bowl in the trashcan in the bathroom, pull the rug off the bed and then replace it with my luxurious Lilly Pulitzer comforter. Looking around I notice the pile of boxes in the corner. It looks like my stuff is here but there is no way I'm unpacking until we get our own place. I don't think anything is going to help the pea green on these walls. I grab my phone to check for messages, but I still don't have service so I put it in my pocket out of habit and walk downstairs for dinner.

The smell of grease hits my nose as I walk into the kitchen. *Gross.* There is a fried chicken with fried potatoes sitting on the counter, and some green beans are sizzling in a pan. Well, backwoods assumption number one has been met. They fry everything.

Taking a plate I neatly arrange the items so they are not touching. Then I take a seat at the table. Gran has poured us a glass of sweet tea. I take a sip and cringe because it tastes like pure syrup. "Gran, do you have any without sugar?"

"Lord no. That's like one of the Ten Commandments. Thou shalt use a stick of butter and a gallon of sugar." Looking at Mom, she nods in agreement.

"Don't you have a salad or grilled chicken?" I ask.

"From the looks of it, I think you could stand to gain a few pounds. You're skin and bones."

"Mother!" Mom jumps in.

"Well, it's the truth, and you could stand a few pounds yourself missy," she says. "Come on. Let's eat."

I take a moment and pray that my teeth are still intact tomorrow and I won't gain ten pounds overnight.

"You know, there's a dance studio about thirty minutes from here. We can go check it out if you like."

"Thanks Gran, but I'm sure they can't compete with my studio in New York."

"Just 'cause we're small town doesn't mean we don't know how to move. You should at least give it a chance."

"We'll see," I say, trying to get Gran to drop the subject. Looking at the chicken, I try to decipher how to eat it. I begin to grab my knife and fork, but Mom clears her throat and I know that's the wrong way so I glance at Mom as she wiggles her fingers. *Seriously?* Placing my napkin in my lap for extra protection, I take a deep breath and delicately take a bite. The grease runs down my cheek, and I have to bite harder to pull the meat away from the bone. Gran starts laughing.

"Cade, you might as well quit worrying about how you're going to stay clean and dig in. If you're having that big of a problem with fried chicken, I hate to see what happens with a rack of ribs."

I try to delicately take another bite, but soon realize it's no use. Grease pops in my mouth and I am so done. I've never tasted such a unique flavor. And grease dripping down my cheek is just gross.

Placing the chicken back on the plate, I decide to remove the crust so it won't be as greasy. I carefully pull the crunchy part from the meat and when the top easily comes off, I feel a sense of accomplishment. Gran takes the crust from my plate and puts it in her mouth.

"That's the best part Cadence," Gran exclaims.

"Doubtful." I take the fork and knife and somehow cut the meat from the bone. Gran stares at me and that pisses me off more while Mom eats quietly. I take small bites and chew them thoroughly in hopes that I'll be full in a few minutes and save myself some calories. As for the tea, I only drink when necessary.

Surprisingly, I finish all of my chicken. It was actually better than a chicken tender, but I'm not going to admit that.

"Gran, where did you buy the chicken?" I ask. Mom pauses, and Gran looks me dead in the eyes.

"Cade, it came from out there." She points toward the back door.

"So the deep freezer?"

"No, the yard. That chicken lived in the barn." I drop the fork, pick up my napkin from my lap and cover my mouth. I try to refrain from vomiting.

"Listen, if you're gonna live here, you're gonna have to get used to a few things. One being that we raise what we eat. The grocery store is thirty minutes down the road, and we don't have any fast food. It's how we live our lives here. You're just going to have to accept it."

"Isn't that like inhumane?" I ask.

"Lord child. You've got a lot to learn. These animals 'round here are treated like royalty. It's the ones you get at McDonald's and those massive farms you have to worry about. No added hormones here. Everything on this farm is grass fed and of the highest quality. You'd be lucky to get this at a grocery store."

"Mom why didn't you tell me?" I whisper.

"What? So you'd starve?" she asks with a smirk.

After we finish eating, Gran asks me to help her with the dishes, and there's no way I'm doing those.

"You're kidding, right?" I say and then walk out of the kitchen.

Taking my phone from my pocket, I hold it in the air as I walk around the house. I open the door and take a step onto the porch. Nothing. I move toward the edge of the porch and it's like winning the lottery. I have a bar and my notifications go crazy.

I dare not move so I stand on the edge and simply read the texts and reply. Nothing from Dad. I don't even know why I got my hopes up. I text Lauren, and as soon as it's delivered she calls me.

"What up Cade?" she asks.

"Girl. You wouldn't believe it if I told you. Oh, service sucks here so I might lose you if I move from this spot."

"How are you going to survive without service?"

"I don't know. So tell me, how was practice today?"

"It was strange without you, but Madame Amy made a few changes to the routine and I think it's going to work as a solo." My heart sinks. That routine isn't supposed to be a solo.

"Oh. Do you like it?" I question with disappointment in my voice.

She pauses and I know she's looking for the right words to say. "It's different. I loved our routine, but this is challenging me as a soloist. Does that make sense?"

"Yeah it does," I say with more attitude than I should.

"Are you mad?"

"I'm not sure. I just left and everyone has already moved on."

"I have not moved on. Do you know how hard it was for me to walk in the studio today? I didn't have my partner in crime to prank Mary Katherine, and when Madame asked for me to come up with an idea for our piece, I drew a blank. I miss you and it's not the same."

Hearing her say those words makes me feel better, but not great. "I'm sorry I was a rude, but today has been awful."

"Tell me what happened."

"For starters, there's no service. I'm literally hanging off the edge of the front porch for one bar. I look like a freaking monkey swinging from a vine. My room is the color of green peas, Gran has dead animals everywhere, and I had to eat fried food."

"Okay, so maybe your room looks like baby poop, but maybe your Gran will let you decorate your room or repaint it. As for the phone service, check to see what the people around there use. I bet there is service but you have the wrong carrier. I mean any kid our age has to have a phone. It's like our heartbeat. I don't know what to tell you about the fried food. I'd just beg for some salad or something."

I smile. Lauren really is my best friend, and even though she's over six hundred miles away I feel like she's with me right now. We talk a few more minutes and laugh about how several of my backwoods assumptions have been correct and come up with a few more.

"I bet everyone is related like they are kissing cousins or something," Lauren says.

"Oh, or maybe everyone's uncle's name is Bubba," I laugh.

"I bet all the girls wear pearls and talk like Scarlett O'Hara."

"That's a good one. I bet they only listen to that awful country music," I add.

We both start to laugh and that's when I hear the screen door open. Gran. "That's enough missy. Get off that phone and in this house this instant."

Rolling my eyes, I continue to talk to Lauren. The next thing I know, Gran takes my phone, politely tells Lauren I will call her later, and then throws it across the yard where it becomes lost in the darkness.

I feel the anger begin to build and just as I'm about to get my revenge, she puts me in my place.

"You listen to me Cadence Mae Lewis. I might not be your mother, but you will listen to me and respect what I have to say in my house."

"Whatever," I huff with another eye roll.

"I'll whatever you into next week if you roll those eyes one more time." I do it again.

"That's it. I was going to offer to take you to the studio down the road this week, but instead, I think you can stay here with me while your mama works."

"Whatever," I say as I move past her. She threw my phone in the yard and there's no way I can find it in the dark. I hurry past Mom and make my way upstairs. *Wait, Mom has a job? Already?* I take a scalding hot shower and crawl into bed while welcoming myself to hell.

5

CADENCE

*O*h my gosh, what is that racket? Bam! Bam! Bam! My bedroom door swings open and Gran is standing there with a wooden spoon and frying pan. It's pitch black outside. I take my pillow and cover my head. Bam! Bam! Baaaammmm! The sound gets louder and before I know it, the pillow has been tossed across the room and she's beating the pan right at my ear.

I cover my ears. "Okay! I get it! I'll get up."

As if she is innocent of the whole wake-up call, she sweetly tells me to put on some old clothes and meet her in the kitchen.

I mumble as I fumble through my boxes attempting to find something old. I don't own anything old. I take a minute to yawn and realize I have old dance clothes. I guess that will just have to do. I put on a pair of booty shorts and a worn out tank. I go to the bathroom and straighten my hair and apply my makeup. I shake my head as I look at myself in the mirror. Looking around for shoes, I have no idea what to put on so I grab a pair of flip-flops and make my way toward the kitchen.

As I enter the kitchen, I'm overcome by the smell of bacon. Here we go again. I take a deep breath and start to choke. I bet I'll smell like grease all day now. Great! Gran has her apron on and is humming a tune and acting as if she wasn't a crazy lady ten minutes ago.

"Mornin' Cadence. Why'd you put all that stuff on?" she questions while gesturing to her face.

"My makeup?" I ask for reassurance and she nods.

"I don't leave home without it."

She shakes her head and I know she's trying to refrain from commenting. "What would you like? I can scramble you an egg if you like."

"Do you have any yogurt?"

"No I have oatmeal. Would you like that?" That actually sounds normal and perfect.

"Please," I say.

"It's in the cabinet. Will you get it for me?"

I walk to the cabinet and take it out. It's just plain. There's no maple sugar and it's in a large container, not a packet. I don't even know what to do with this. Gran giggles.

"I can add some syrup to it. No worries. I don't like it plain either. My favorite is peanut butter and honey. You should try it." That actually does sound great. Not to mention it's full of protein. I take her up on her offer and take a seat.

Mom joins us while I'm still trying to figure out why I had to get up so early.

Mom looks toward me. "Cadence, I'm starting a job today. I'll be leaving in the next hour." I guess Gran did know what she was talking about.

"Excuse me? How did you get a job? We just got here."

"I'm working for a local paper in Hickory. I accepted the offer yesterday over the phone."

"A local newspaper? Mom, you worked for one of the most successful fashion magazines in New York! What's up with that? Can't you work freelance for them or just use the money Dad's sending you? This is all his fault anyway."

"Cadence! I'm a grown woman, and I have my own money. I will not touch a dime of your father's. Besides the market is different here. It might be a nice change of pace."

"What am I going to do?" I question, no longer feeling hungry.

"I believe Gran told you last night."

"Me? Work on a farm? Um, no thanks," I say forcing another bite of oatmeal.

Mom puts her fork down and I know I'm in trouble. She points her finger at me. "Yes you will help Gran. Do you understand me?"

"Fine," I say, but that doesn't mean I have to do it willingly.

After we finish eating, Gran tells me to get her old brown boots by the door. I laugh because they are no longer brown but a light tan and I'm sure both of my feet could fit in one.

BARRICK

While driving to Ms. Mae's, I wonder how her evening went. She was not herself yesterday. She seemed to be going above and beyond to make everything perfect. She never tries to impress anyone. What you see is what you get with her and I admire that.

As I pull into the driveway, the first thing I notice is a top-of-the-line Chevrolet with New York tags. It's so shiny and new, I bet it's got all the bells and whistles on it. *Who does Ms. Mae know in New York?* I park my truck and make my way into the barn. I feed the horses, and check the equipment before bringing the cows in for milking. After I've finished a round, I hear the barn door open.

"Ms. Mae?" I call out.

"Yes, Barrick. I've got someone I'd like you to meet."

"Hold on. Let me finish with this set and I'll be there in just a sec…" I don't finish my words because as I glance up, I see more than Ms. Mae. I see a girl with long blond hair in perfect makeup wearing workout clothes and a pair of boots that are way too big for her. I sure hope she's not expecting to stay clean around here. She has bold eyes that are staring right at me. I quickly stand from my stool and wipe my hands on my jeans.

"Barrick, I wanted to introduce you to my granddaughter, Cadence. She and her mom, Regina, are going to be staying here awhile. She's going to help us out until school starts and maybe a little while longer."

I look at her and am in awe of her beauty, but yet want to laugh at the fact that it's obvious this is something she's never done before and the look on her face is priceless. I extend my hand to introduce myself. "Barrick, nice to meet you." She stands there with her arms crossed and looks at me like I've lost my mind.

"Um, you were just holding that cow's boob over there. Do you really think I'm going to shake your hand?" she says with disdain.

I ignore her and look toward Ms. Mae. "I've finished with the first group of cows, and fed the horses. I hope to be finished milking the others by seven-thirty. Anything new on the agenda for today?"

"I know the stalls need to be cleaned and new hay added. Cadence is going to help you with that today. Also, we need to check the garden, and start a plan for when you pick up those other two classes at the community college."

"Yes ma'am," I say as I smile toward Cadence and go back to work. Ms. Mae shows her around the barn, but I can't concentrate. All I can see is the way her bottom fits those stretch shorts a little too well, and how Ms. Mae's old boots are two sizes too big. This is going to be interesting.

6

CADENCE

*S*he did not say I'm cleaning out cow poop. There's no way! Gran gives me a tour of the barn and tells me we are going to take a ride on the Gator. What in the world? I'm not a zookeeper. As she leads me outside, I see a funky looking golf cart. It's missing a front window and it has storage in the back. I take a seat next to her and in bright yellow is the word Gator. *Oh! I got it!* Gran turns the key and starts the ignition. Within seconds I know this is better than a golf cart because it goes faster than a snail's pace. She points out all of the different areas of the farm and what they do each day. So far, I've seen cows, horses, a small pond, pigs, chickens, and a garden. The only thing that continues to stand out in my mind is Barrick. I'm not sure why, but something about him pisses me off. He has this attitude about him like he's perfect or something.

Arriving back at the barn, Gran remains seated. I stand, and she tells me to have a seat.

"Why?" I question.

"Cadence, it's too early for this nonsense. Have a seat," she says.

"I'm good standing."

"Suit yourself. Today you are going to help Barrick clean the stalls."

"What? I don't know how to do that," I say crossing my arms. "Why can't you do it?"

"I have a few calls to make about pick up and deliveries."

"It's not hard. After you finish that we will start in the garden. I don't want the sun to get up too high or we're liable to have a stroke out here."

"What did you say? A stroke?" I ask with concern and confusion.

"Not literally. If you haven't noticed it's hot and sticky here, makes you feel like you're a stick of butter melting. I can promise that you don't want to be out here in the heat of the day, but if you don't get to moving, you will be."

"I'm not doing any of it Gran. This is *not* what I signed up to do."

"Sugar, the moment you disrespected me was the moment I knew it was time to teach you a lesson or two about life. So pick up those boots and march your butt right in there."

Looking towards the pasture, I notice my cell phone lodged in a pile of crap.

"Gran, my phone! It landed in a pile of crap."

"Well, brush it off."

"Oh, no, I'm not touching that and now I need a new phone. How am I going to talk to Lauren and my other friends without a phone?"

"I have one in the house. Now quit your whining and get started on those stalls."

Reluctantly, I follow Gran into the barn. Hearing a crazy sound, I have no idea what I'm about to do, but I pray it doesn't have anything to do with a cow's tatas.

BARRICK

Over the sound of the milking machine, I can hear Ms. Mae. She's giving that girl an earful and then I hear Cadence fire back. That girl doesn't know when to shut up. I'd love to take a piece of duct tape to her mouth. Doesn't she know Ms. Mae is her grandma and she's supposed to respect her? I shake my head as I hear the barn door slide open. I stand there knowing I have a few more minutes until it's time to remove the cups from the udders.

"Barrick, I've got to make a few phone calls. Cadence is going to help you in the stalls. Isn't that right?" she says, looking at Cadence. I want to laugh, but I know better. Ms. Mae would chew me out.

"I guess," Cadence replies.

"Now you listen to Barrick and do what he tells ya. You hear me?" Ms. Mae says to her and as she's about to comment, Ms. Mae cuts her off. "And don't you 'whatever' me either missy!" I cough to try and cover my laugh.

Ms. Mae leaves us alone in the barn, and Cadence stands there with her arms crossed with her weight all on her right side. I know I shouldn't think this, but she's hot when she's pissed off. Maybe I should try and piss her off more? *Nah? Well, maybe. It could be fun.*

"Cadence, right?" I question.

"Yup."

"I've got a few more minutes with this last set of cows, and then I need to clean up before we get started. So follow me," I say as politely as possible.

Glancing over my shoulder I see that she hasn't moved. "Are you comin' or what?"

"No, and nobody's gonna make me either."

"Whatever, isn't that your word?" I smart off to her.

"What's that supposed to mean?" she asks, getting defensive.

"It means you're too good to get your hands dirty and to respect what Ms. Mae has asked you to do. Where did you come from?"

"New York," she says with a smile.

"Well, you need to learn to use something called manners. I know you got 'em."

She gives a huff and another whatever, but finally follows me into the milking room.

"Can you go and turn that pump off?" I ask, pointing to a switch by the pump.

Reluctantly, she walks over to the pump, and stares. "It's right there." I point again, and she doesn't do anything. Knowing it needs to be stopped as soon as the milking is done, I move from the cow and walk toward her. Just as I reach her, she turns the switch. *You've got to be kidding me. So this is how we're going to play?*

I calmly walk back to the cow and look at the others that need to have their cups removed. She's only supposed to clean stalls, but why not show her what it's all about.

"Cadence, come here a second. Let me show you something." She rolls her eyes and walks to me. "Let me show you how to take the cups off."

"Um, no. That is not what Gran asked me to do."

"I believe she said you had to do as I asked, and you might need to learn since you're helping out."

"How about I watch instead?"

"Fine, but if I know Ms. Mae, this is in your future," I say while removing the cups.

The look on her face was pure disgust. Once I finish removing the cups, I lead the cows into the pasture. Knowing I have to clean the lines before the next round of milking this afternoon, I decide to go ahead and show Cadence how to clean the stalls.

"I've got to clean up in here, but let me show you how to clean the stalls. When I finish I'll come and help."

Walking to the stall closest to the entrance, I grab two pitchforks and hand one to her.

"Cadence, we need to scoop the manure and place it in this wheelbarrow. Once that's finished, check for any urine. The smell can get pretty bad so we spray a solution to neutralize it. Once that is finished, we add fresh hay to the stall. Think you got it?"

"Yeah, doesn't sound like rocket science."

"Great, I'm going to clean up then I'll help you."

She takes her pitchfork and steps in the stall. I give her five minutes before she's crying like a baby.

CADENCE

There's no way I'm going to let some country backwoods boy think he can do this better than me. I take my pitchfork and walk into the stall. It smells terrible in here. Looking down I know why. I start to laugh, I'm in Delight, also known as hades, with a pitchfork and it smells like a sewer. I guess it can't get any worse than this.

I take the pitchfork and stab it into the ground. As I lift it, I realize it's a lot heavier than I thought. I turn to toss it into the wheelbarrow, but as soon as I turn the pitchfork over half of it falls back onto the ground. Trying it again, I scoop it up, and place it in there perfectly. I continue at a steady pace until I'm at the last pile. As I pick it up I'm horrified. I scream louder than I ever have in my life, drop the pitchfork and quickly run out of the stall and straight into Barrick.

"What's wrong?" he asks calmly.

"Big. Nasty. Slimy." I stutter as he looks at me like I'm crazy. He looks over my shoulder and investigates the situation.

"Oh you met Rascal, the black snake."

"You mean to tell me he's a pet?" I question.

"Kinda. He's welcome here. He keeps the varmints away."

"Well, this girl doesn't do snakes," I say as I point to myself and walk toward the door.

"It won't hurt ya. I promise," he yells behind me.

"I don't do snakes," I yell back as I slide the door open and walk toward the house.

7

BARRICK

*W*hen I heard Cadence scream, I thought she was bleeding or something. It never even crossed my mind that Rascal was hiding out in that stall. In fact, my heart was beating so hard before I got there, I thought if something had happened to her that I'd never forgive myself. Not to mention that Ms. Mae would probably kill me.

I tried to act as if it was no big deal, but that didn't go over very well with her. She stormed out of here like she was on fire. I can't imagine what she's telling Ms. Mae. Knowing I don't need to worry about it, I finish cleaning the equipment, and start working on the stalls.

I'm about halfway through the stalls when I hear the door slide open again. I don't pause; I just continue to work as I would any other day. I hear someone clear their throat. As I wipe the sweat from my brow, I look over my shoulder and see Cadence.

"So you're back," I state nicely.

"Unfortunately," she replies, taking a seat on the wooden stool.

"I don't know why you're sitting down because there are four more stalls to go."

"I told you I wasn't cleaning stalls and I meant it," she says with her legs and arms crossed.

"Fine," I say as I prop my pitchfork against the wall. "If you don't want to do this then how about you take that wheelbarrow full of cow manure to the compost pile."

"The what?" she asks, standing from the stool.

"Take it to that pile behind the fence line. It's a compost pile. It's a way to reuse waste."

"So I take this wheelbarrow and dump it back there?" I nod. "Well, that doesn't look too hard."

"Then have at it." She rolls her eyes, and makes her way out of the barn. "Oh, here's a pair of gloves for you so you don't ruin those pretty hands of yours."

She snatches them from me, and I can't wait to see how this is going to play out. I finish cleaning the stall and decide to watch her for a moment. Little does she know we always use the bucket on the tractor to make this a super easy job. Peering out the door, she's almost to the fence line. She's made pretty good time getting down there, probably due to the fact that she's in killer shape, but when she attempts to dump the manure it doesn't go as easy as she planned. I watch her try over and over again to spill the contents into the pile. Then she begins to swat at something, and before I know it, she lands right in the middle of a huge pile of compost. I bite my lip to refrain from laughing, but it's no use. I double over and take a step back inside the barn. When I gather myself together, I go back to finish the other stalls and wait for the storm that's about to enter in three, two, one.

CADENCE

Just as I've almost gotten the manure in the manure pile I lose my flippin' balance. Dang these boots! I scream from irritation and look straight toward the barn. I bet Barrick knew this was going to happen. I stand and as I take a step I slip and fall yet again.

Take.

A.

Deep.

Breath.

Yeah right! I huff and start on a mission to give Barrick yet another piece of my mind. With the wheelbarrow in tow, I march back to the barn. I drop it loudly and startle him, but I can already see the joke's on me.

"So wasn't so easy was it?" he asks.

"Guess you could say that. I'm going to shower before I help Gran in the garden."

"No need darlin', she can use you as fertilizer," he says with a wink. *Did he just wink?*

I dust the manure off of my shoulder and walk toward the house with my head held high.

As I approach, I can see that Gran is already in the garden. I decide to suck it up and deal with this crap, literally.

"Lord have mercy child. What happened to ya?" Gran asks, looking me up and down.

"Your boy down there had me take the cow poop to the compost pile and you can see the crap won," I say with my arms outstretched.

"Bless your heart. Didn't you use the tractor?"

"Tractor?" At that exact moment I hear an engine and I can't believe what I'm seeing. Barrick is using a bucket to haul the rest of the manure down there. He looks toward us and waves. It's on like Donkey Kong.

"Oh, Cadence, I'm sorry. Why don't you go get a shower?"

For the first time, I can see that Gran is acting like a caring individual rather than a tough, country woman trying to teach me a lesson.

"But first, can you dust some of that off right here in the garden?" I start to open my mouth to say something very inappropriate. "I'm just joking. Go get a shower. I'll be in shortly."

I turn to make my way inside, but stop to glance down toward the barn once more. It's so on.

8

CADENCE

*A*fter showering, I go downstairs and give Lauren a call on Gran's landline. I just need a moment to vent. She can't believe anything that I'm telling her. I should have taken a picture of myself for proof. Um no, that could be used as blackmail.

"So he's making your life hard?" Lauren asks.

"Not just him, Gran too. She told me that I had to be *respectful* before she even thinks about taking me to a studio. Not to mention Mom's already gotten a job, and there's no way I can leave this place."

"Since your Gran decided to go easy on you for the rest of the day, why don't you enjoy it."

"How do you expect me to do that, Lauren?"

"Watch a little TV, maybe even dance outside, or maybe you should plot your revenge."

"I like it! Go on."

"Well, why not do stuff to him? He thinks he's got the upper hand, but watch him a day or so. Find out his habits and then strike."

"Yeah like Rascal! I think maybe I could come up with a few

things." With Lauren's comments the wheels begin to spin in my mind. "Thanks. I swear. I'm almost ready for school to start because at least I won't have to work around here, but revenge could give me a reason to wake up each morning."

"That's my girl! Well, I gotta run. Call me soon!" We say our good-byes and hang up.

After walking around the house contemplating what I should do, I decide to take a seat on the couch and watch TV for a little while. It doesn't take long before I decide that local channels aren't going to cut it so I start to think of ways to prank Barrick. Eventually, I decide to push that to the side because until I learn his daily routine, I'm wasting time. Tomorrow I'm going to be a good little girl on the farm and do as I'm told. Let's see how good I can fake it.

Deciding that a good story might clear my mind, I look at the shelves of books Gran has in her living room. Most are worn, and look like they have been read multiple times. I can't help wishing there was a great dystopian novel amongst them. As my finger drags over the spines, I pause on a John Grisham novel, and pull it from the others. Looks interesting, so I take it, plop down on the couch and open it up.

I have no idea when Gran entered the house, but as the sound of a mixer echoes throughout the house, I know it must be close to lunchtime. Putting the book on the end table, I stand and go see what's to eat. I'm completely shocked when I see her with a glass of green mixture.

"Gran what's that?" I ask.

"A green shake. I was going to fix you a sandwich and chips, but I thought this might be more up your alley."

Taking the glass from her, I'm surprised she would know the ingredients in a green shake. I take a sip and am unsure. It's nothing like the shake at the smoothie shop. It's actually better. There's a crispness to it and it has a bit of a tart taste.

"Gran, this is good! What did you put in here?" I ask as I take another sip.

"Oh anything and everything from the garden, plus two fresh squeezed lemons. That's the secret." She winks.

"How do you know about these?"

"I saw an infomercial on some fancy smoothie machine. I thought to myself, I bet I can make that and make it taste better. Now, it took a little bit of trial and error, but I like them when it's hot like this. Plus, I know I'm getting all the vegetables this old lady needs."

"I'm glad I wasn't here for the trial and error part!" I laugh and she does too.

"I'm going to take mine to the porch. Would you like to come sit with me?"

"Sure."

Gran and I walk outside to the porch, and it's ridiculously hot. Sweat begins to bead on my forehead and as we are about to sit down, I see him coming. *Great.*

"Gran, I think I'm going to go inside and finish this."

"But Cadence, we just got out here," she says patting the seat.

"Nah, I'd rather not," I say and cut my eyes toward Barrick as his foot lands on the top step.

BARRICK

"Ms. Mae, I've finished down at the barn for now. Is there anything in the garden that needs pickin'?" I ask as Cadence hurries inside like someone lit her on fire. I shake my head.

"No, I don't believe so. I know tomorrow we'll need to get ready for the farmers' market, and if you're wanting to dove hunt in a few weeks, feel free to get the field ready on your down time."

"Thanks. Smoothie for lunch again today?" I ask. God I hate those things.

"Actually, since I know those aren't your favorite, there's stuff for tomato sandwiches and even a fresh loaf of homemade sourdough."

"Awesome. Thanks," I say as I begin to open the screen door.

"Oh and Barrick, you two try not to start a fire while you're in there please."

"Yes ma'am."

Walking into the house, I glance to the left and see Cadence lying on the couch with a book and her smoothie. I ignore her and make my way to the kitchen. I quickly make myself a sandwich, chips, and glass of sweet tea and sit at the table. It feels good to sit down inside. The air is definitely not cold by any means, but it's significantly cooler than outside.

I take out my cellphone and check social media and my text messages while I eat. Standing to get a napkin with my phone in my hand, I run into Cadence.

"Where did you get that?" she asks, staring at my phone like it's a million dollars.

"The store?" I reply, confused.

"Does it work here?"

"Um, yeah." Why else would I be using it?

"You've got to help me get one."

I grab a napkin, and turn to look at her again. "Can you repeat that?" I ask with a smile.

"Don't get any ideas, cowboy. I had one till Gran threw it across the yard, but it didn't work half the time here anyway. So, are you going to help me or what?" she asks while standing with her hands on her hips.

"Depends. Does Ms. Mae want you to have one?"

"Ohmygosh! What are you, like perfect or something? I've got money. Not to mention a mother as well. I just have no way out of this place so are you going to help me or what?"

"No, I'm not a goodie-goodie, but I do what's asked of me. So if you aren't allowed then no, I'm not helping you. If you can, I'll be glad to. I can get one when I go in town for the farmers' market. You just have to get the okay from Ms. Mae or your mama."

She gets quiet on that comment. I'm not sure if it's because a phone is off limits or what, but I already know this girl is accustomed to getting exactly what she wants.

9

CADENCE

I have a glimmer of hope that things are looking up after my conversation with Barrick. It's the first time since I've arrived that something might go my way. I don't have my contacts backed up but I know the few numbers that matter, and everyone else can give me a like, tweet, or comment. It's at least a start.

Gran enters through the creaky screen door off the porch.

"Shew! It's hot as sin out there!" she says and I totally agree.

"So Gran what are you going to do the rest of the day?" I question.

"Right now, it's time for my stories then I'll check on Barrick in the barn after the next round of milkin'. You might want to go with me for that."

"I think I'll pass," I respond but quickly change my tune when I remember I need to start playing the game. "Well, I guess. If that's what you want."

"I think that would be very nice of you."

After Gran finishes watching her stories, we walk out to the barn to check on Barrick.

Hearing the pumps as we enter the barn makes my boobs hurt. That's got to hurt. Barrick is standing between two cows and once he finishes he looks our way.

"How's it going?" Gran asks.

"Like clockwork, Ms. Mae. I'm just finishing up," Barrick says with a smile.

"Great! Cadence and I just stopped by to see if you were done. Will you be here early tomorrow?"

"Yes ma'am," I reply.

"Cadence, tomorrow morning you are to help Barrick at the farmers' market. He will tend to the cows then you will make your way into town."

"Yes, Gran." They both look at me for a beat and then Gran continues with her instructions for market day.

Once Gran is finished with the details, she excuses me from the barn. I walk toward the house, and notice that the sun isn't quite as high and behind a few clouds. I decide to grab my iPod and dance out on the back porch. I turn on a classical piece with a modern twist. It's sweet yet angry, and fits my mood perfectly. I stretch, flex, and move to the beat as I count in my head. This is the first piece of heaven I've had since I left New York.

BARRICK

Ms. Mae goes over a few other items with me, and I try my best to listen but all I can think about is Cadence's reaction to her tasks tomorrow. It seems like she's trying, but why? Earlier this morning she was determined to not getting any dirt under her nails. It makes absolutely no sense to me at all, but then it hits me, she wants that phone.

When Ms. Mae finishes, I gather as much as I can for tomorrow. Market days are long and tiring so I want to have my truck loaded and ready to go after I'm done milking the cows in the morning. I make sure the milking equipment is ready to go and then begin to load my truck.

As I'm covering the back, I hear music but don't know where it's coming from. I look around and that's when I see Cadence moving to the music on the back porch. I stop in my tracks. I can't take my eyes off of her. The way her body sways and moves is like wheat moving in the wind. She's graceful yet edgy. As the song begins to fade, I stop staring and walk back in the barn to close up, but all I can see is Cadence moving to the music. I feel like I caught a glimpse of the real Cadence that's behind the wall she puts up.

10

CADENCE

*A*t four o'clock in the morning, my alarm begins to buzz. I wish I could sleep for five more minutes or the rest of the day but then I remember what today is. It's the first day of making Barrick's life miserable. I smile, toss my covers off, and let my feet touch the cool wooden floor. I hurry to the bathroom, check the mirror and realize I have no clue what to wear to the farmers' market. Maybe Mom will know. I tiptoe into her room, and wake her.

"Cadence, are you okay? It's four in the morning," she says with a yawn.

"I'm fine. I've got to work the farmers' market today. What do I wear?" I whisper.

"Whatever you want. It will be hot though."

Well, that's not a lot of direction, but I guess I'll work with it. I go to my closet, and pull a tank top with an embellished neckline and a pair of matching shorts. Then I look through my shoes and pull out a pair of sandals. How hard can this be? I mean, we are just selling vegetables.

I take a few extra minutes to perfectly apply my makeup and straighten my hair. I brush my teeth and then smile in the mirror. Let's do this.

As I enter the kitchen, Gran hands me another green smoothie, and I thank her, take a seat, and get my game face on. Mom comes downstairs in her pajamas.

"Why are you up?" I ask.

"Well, let's just say I had an early wake up call, and now I can't sleep. No worries." She pours a cup of coffee and turns to face me. "We've got to get you some new clothes."

"What do you mean?" I ask.

She shakes her head and takes a seat at the table with me, and it gives me the perfect opportunity to ask about the phone.

"So Mom, can I get a new phone when I'm in town?"

She puts her cup down and looks at Gran. Is she looking for a blessing?

"Cadence, I doubt a cellphone will work out here."

"Mom, Barrick has one and it works. I saw it. Pleassseeee!" I beg.

"Fine. Don't get some crazy plan with crazy charges."

"Thanks Mom!" I say as I put my glass in the sink and grab a cup of black coffee for the road.

Walking toward the barn, I see that Barrick has already arrived. I slide the door open and hear the machines. Yuck! I take a deep breath and walk toward him.

"Morning Barrick," I say as pleasantly as possible. He looks up at me.

"Morning. Um, can you do me a favor and put those last two baskets on the back of my truck?"

I pause, afraid it might be another joke after the compost pile incident.

As if he's reading my mind he says, "I promise it's legit. That's how you're supposed to do it."

I smile and make my way to them. Good gosh these are heavy. As I approach the truck, I try to decide the best way to accomplish this task. I'm not tall enough to lift and place the basket over. Carefully, I pull the lever to open the tailgate so that nothing tumbles out.

Once I'm in the clear, I slide the basket in and turn to get the last one. Barrick meets me at the barn door with it in his arms.

"Thank you for grabbing the last one," I say with a smile.

"No problem," he says, skeptically. Lord, I hope he's not on to me.

I walk to the passenger side, and am pleasantly surprised by the amount of room in this truck and how clean it is. It's not like Gran's at all. Our ride to the farmers' market is relatively quiet except for the radio in the background.

Once we arrive, Barrick pulls into his assigned spot but pauses a moment before getting out of the truck. "Cadence, this place is crazy. Just try to keep up and pay attention to what I do especially with the prices and such." Seriously, does he think I'm an idiot? I try to refrain from rolling my eyes, but it's no use. I do however wait until his back is turned.

By eight o'clock, cars are beginning to arrive and the sun is high in the sky. We've set up our table, unloaded, and I'm sweating like crazy. I try to gracefully wipe it from my brow when Barrick sees me.

"There's a towel in my truck or a hat if you want. It's only going to get worse," he says.

"Thanks, but I'm good for right now. Is there a restroom?" I question and he points across the market. I excuse myself and when I open the restroom door, I'm hit with heat and funk. I hurry to handle my business. When I look in the mirror I want to die! I look horrible! Taking a paper towel, I blot my face and try to salvage what makeup is left on my face. Not to mention that my eyeliner smudged and Barrick didn't bother to tell me. Boys! I walk back to our table that is now overflowing with customers.

"Cadence, can you grab another basket of tomatoes?" he asks as I approach. I tell him yes and then begin to help him with the rest of the orders.

As noon approaches, I'm absolutely exhausted and my hair looks a mess. I don't even need a mirror to prove it. It's stringy, knotty, and makes me feel as if it's twenty degrees hotter.

"Cadence, I'm telling ya. Grab my hat, it will help." I don't want his help, but at this point I'm dying from the heat. I walk toward the truck and find it. Ewww, camo? It does not match my outfit. As I bring it toward my head, I smell something and realize that it's the hat. Nope, can't do it. There's got to be something else. Why didn't I grab a hair tie this morning?

"Did you find it?" he questions.

"Yeah. I'm not wearing that! It doesn't match my outfit and it stinks!" I say with spice, and just like that my game face is broken. I poke around in his back seat, and am completely surprised when I find a rubber band. This is going to break my hair but I've got to do something. I close the door and look in the side mirror while I pull it up into a cute yet messy bun. Perfect!

BARRICK

What is she doing? So what if the hat's camo and it stinks? It's a hat for crying out loud. I try not to worry about her and focus on the customers. I finish ringing up an elderly couple and turn to see what she's doing. As I turn around, she's right in front of me with her hair pulled up in some creative bird's nest and a smile. I hate to admit it, but she looks hot. Her makeup is barely visible, her cheeks are flushed from the heat, and her smile looks genuine.

"I found a rubber band. Guess it will have to do," she says, and I know she's right because it does exactly what it should and more.

A little after lunch the crowd begins to dwindle and we begin to pack up what few items we have left.

I can tell that as much as Cadence has tried to act like she's okay with being here, she hates every minute of it. Glancing at my watch, I know it's time to go, and I'm starving.

"You ready?" I ask her.

"I guess. So was it a good day?" she questions.

"Yeah it was. We've been working on bringing just enough, and this week we only have half a basket left."

"What are we going to do with it?"

"We're going to drop it off at the battered women's shelter before we go back to the farm, and then we're going to get some real food for lunch."

"Oh, and by real food what do you mean?" she asks.

"Not a dang green shake. Here we have plenty of choices. There's anything from burgers, pizza, salads, seafood, or anything else you might like. What would you like?" I say trying to be nice, but knowing I'm getting a Blizzard before I go back for sure.

"I don't know. I'm more of a green shake kind of girl," she says with a wink.

"Do you eat anything bad for you?" I ask her, genuinely concerned.

"Well, I'm a sucker for froyo."

"Okay, well, we don't have froyo around here, but we have the best Blizzards."

"A what?" she says, confused.

"You've never been to a Dairy Queen?" I ask. That should be a sin itself.

"Nope. Never heard of it," she says.

"Dairy Queen it is. You can even get a salad there, but you have to order a Blizzard. You've got to live a little," I say while shaking my head.

CADENCE

Barrick drives to the shelter, and I go in with him to deliver the fresh produce. I'm accustomed to seeing people down and out as I walk in town. What I'm not used to is seeing people so gracious for a handout. Most people I've come across beg for money. These people are the opposite. They are thankful for what is handed to them and you can see that Gran's help does make a difference.

"You ready?" Barrick asks as we get back in the truck. I'm scared. What is he talking about?

"For what?" I say as I look at him like he's lost his mind.

"Dairy Queen." Food, go figure, but the only thing on my mind is a phone.

"What about that promise you made?" I question and he looks puzzled. "My phone," I say.

"Oh, you sure it was okay?" he asks and I really want to just smack him.

"Yes, do you want to call Gran to double check?" I sass back.

"Nah, I believe ya," he says with a laugh, and that pisses me off.

"What's so funny?" I ask as I face him.

"You. That's what's funny. Most people are worried about eating and stuff, but not you. You just need a lifeline to yankeeville."

"Whatever," I say.

He turns to look at me. "Seriously, can't you stop with that 'whatever' mess? It's not attractive on a girl at all."

Hold up, did he just call me attractive or say I wasn't attractive?

"Excuse me?"

"Do you really need me to spell it out for you? Whatever is one of those words to try and make yourself look like you're better or you know more information when actually you don't know anything. It makes you look stupid."

"I am *not* stupid!" I yell at him as he drives down the road.

"Never said you were, but it makes you appear that way," he says as he pulls into a parking lot. "We're here." He opens the door but I don't move. "You comin' or what?" he questions.

"Nope," I say with my arms folded.

"Suit yourself," he says as he takes the keys and walks inside. The heat begins to rise and so does my temper. How dare he leave me out here? Who does he think he is? Is he really eating it inside? When I can no longer stand the sauna of the truck, I push open the door and stomp across the parking lot and swing open the door to find him seated in front of a big TV watching baseball highlights. He looks up at me when I reach the table.

"I didn't know what you'd want, but I got you a grilled chicken salad with Italian dressing. Oh and dirty water. I mean an unsweetened tea," he says with a disgusting look on his face.

Sliding into the booth, I don't say a word. Instead, I pop the plastic lid off the salad, and dip my fork in the dressing then my salad. Dressing is full of too many calories.

As I wipe my lips with my napkin, I can't help but stare at him as he eats a greasy burger. I want to say it looks disgusting, but for the first time in my life, I really want a bite. What is wrong with me?

He catches me staring. "Wanna bite?" he asks, pushing the burger toward me.

"I'm good. I can't eat that."

"Why? It's just a burger."

"I only eat turkey burgers. They have less fat and calories."

He places his burger back on the wrapper and wipes his fingers. "Cadence, I don't know why you're worried. You're in perfect shape. One burger won't kill ya. I promise," he says, and the way he's built I think I could agree.

"I'm good."

"You are getting dessert. What's your favorite? Oreo, Nerds, Reese's, or strawberry cheesecake?" he questions.

"Um, Oreo," I say, even though it's been years since I've eaten one. "But I want a small one."

Barrick excuses himself and then comes back to his seat empty-handed. "Where are they?" I question. He places a number on the table, and within minutes a worker brings them to the table.

Looking down at the small cup, I see death by calories and chocolate. He smiles, and I pick up my spoon and place the cool chocolate ice cream into my mouth. It's sweet and the Oreos are crunchy. This is perfection.

The look on my face must say it all because Barrick begins to laugh. "That good huh?" he questions.

"It's okay," I say, refusing to give him the win.

BARRICK

Watching Cadence try and act like I wasn't right was one of the cutest things I've ever seen. We finish and walk toward the truck. After we purchase her new cellphone, I no longer have her attention. She spends every moment downloading apps and sending text messages. She laughs as she continues to talk to someone, and I wonder whom it might be.

As we arrive back at the farm, the first thing she does is pull down the visor and check her makeup and hair. I try not to laugh out loud.

"What's so funny?" she questions.

"You've worked all day in the heat, got your nice clothes dirty, and you're still worried about your makeup and hair. I don't get it."

She rolls her eyes, "You wouldn't. You're a guy."

"Good point. Look, thanks for giving today a shot. I've got to start milkin' again. Would you mind grabbing the empty baskets and placing them in the barn?"

She cuts her eyes toward me, "I think I can handle it."

Ms. Mae has already started milking the cows. I tell her she didn't have to do that, and give her the money from today. She thanks me and calls for Cadence to thank her as well. She also thanks us for working together, and then excuses herself and I finish the job.

The entire time I'm working, I keep thinking about Cadence and how her attitude was different. It was nice that she wasn't so difficult today. I wonder if that is the real Cadence and if the snarky one will be back tomorrow. I guess I'll find out tomorrow when I have her milk the cows.

11

CADENCE

*O*h my gosh, I can't wait to take a shower. I'm sticky, hot, smell like dirt, and ate way too much junk today. Walking into the house, my phone dings and I get a thrill of excitement. I have service! Yes! I spend the remainder of the afternoon making myself feel brand new again as well as talking to Lauren between her classes. She calls me after dinner and I fill her in on today's adventures, and she tells me she needs a picture of Barrick. I tell her I'll see what I can do before hanging up and going to bed.

My alarm goes off at four. *What the world? I forgot to set it for six.* I quickly reset it and roll back over, but I hear Gran and Mom talking loudly in the hall. All I can make out is dance and respect. Maybe just maybe, she'll take me to that hillbilly studio today, I mean anything is better than milking cows and cleaning stalls all day. My hopes are dashed when I hear Gran tell Mom she will not until school starts.

I shake my head, check the clock, and doze back off until I have to either get myself up or wake up to the sound of a clanging frying pan. I'm choosing my alarm.

I throw on some old dance clothes and walk downstairs to get the day started. I'm hoping to get some time to myself today so I can dance. I see Gran's boots sitting at the door and know that I'm going to have to get some 'old' clothes and some boots of my own. I just pray I don't fall in them again today.

After breakfast, I text Lauren and tell her it's time to put my plan in action. Knowing Barrick can't hear anything over those machines, I walk to his truck and turn the switch one turn before finding a heavy metal station and turning it up as loud as possible. I kill the switch and walk into the barn with a smile.

"Mornin' Cadence," Barrick says as he's milking a cow. Let me show you how this works in case you ever have to help." I want to run right back into the house, but I know I've got to play nice. I slowly walk toward him. "Honestly, it's not that hard, and you don't have to touch the teat if you don't want to."

"The what?" I ask.

"Boob, tata, breast, yabos…" he explains.

I cover my face. "Oh my gosh. I can't do this. I just can't," I plead.

"Yeah you can. Come here. I finished with Daisy." He bends down and I have to admit I watch his backside more than his hands. "Just take this metal cup and remove the suction. Then it just falls off. See, it's easy," he says.

"Right," I say with my arms crossed.

"Try it," he says. I hesitate. "Come on. Don't be a chicken."

"Fine," I say as I take a step forward. He stands behind me and tells me what to do. I try to grab the cup but move back quickly. I cannot touch a cow's boob. I just can't. After the third time of me going back and forth, I feel Barrick behind me. He takes his hand and grazes my arm until he finds my hand and assists me. I hold my breath and within a second it's over. I did it. I removed the cup without touching a cow.

"Good job. Now try the next one by yourself."

"I don't know," I say, unsure.

"You just did it. No worries." I nod and take a deep breath.

I bend toward the cow's girl parts and as I place my hand on the cups and pull, the cow begins to moo. I jump, turn and scream right into Barrick's arms.

"Ohmygosh! Ohmygosh! Ohmygosh! I'm done." I squirm as he bursts out laughing.

"I wish I had that on video. That would go viral." He keeps laughing and now I'm pissed. Yeah, you just wait until later today, I think to myself.

"Ughhhh!" I smack him on the shoulder and take a seat in the corner farthest from the cow.

BARRICK

That had to have been the funniest thing I've seen in a long time. Who am I kidding? That's the funniest thing since Cadence landed in cow manure. I tried my best to keep it together but when she started running and jumping and hollering I couldn't help it. I'm surprised the cows didn't go ballistic.

Cadence refuses to help me, and I'm not surprised. I knew her pleasant attitude yesterday had to be a fluke. Why did I think she had changed? She's only been here a few days. It will take a lot longer than that to remove the stick up her butt. She watches me as I work and I can't stand the prissy attitude anymore. She needs to either help or get out. When I see that she has no intention of helping the rest of the day, I suggest that she go help Ms. Mae in the garden.

12

CADENCE

*B*arrick dismissed me, so I huff and leave to go find Gran. She is sitting on the back porch and she smiles and hands me a bucket as I reach her. I take it in my hands and quietly follow her out into the garden of the unknown. I mean what's next? So far this week I've played in poop, got scared by a snake, touched a cow's boob, and had to spend all day with Barrick at a farmers' market.

"Cadence, why don't you start right there with green beans." She walks to the other aisle and begins to pick one. "If they are about this size," she says, holding one up for me to see, "pick them, if not, leave them alone. They should be good in another few days."

"Okay." I take my time picking them to try and reduce the amount of sweat that is seeping out of my skin. The sun is not high in the sky, but this stickiness is killing me. "Gran, why's it so sticky here? I mean, I walk outside and start to sweat."

"It's called humidity, and it's not going away anytime soon."

We remain quiet, and I finish with my row and start another. When my bucket is full, I ask Gran what I should do next. She tells me to take it to the back porch and grab another one. I do, and when I return Gran asks me to start on the cucumbers. I feel semi-confident that this isn't rocket science so I decide to start without instruction. I walk down the row and when I find one, I pull it. "Ouch!" I yell as I shake my right hand as if it's on fire. Gran pauses and looks at me.

She begins to laugh, and I'm starting to get annoyed with everyone laughing at me. "Cadence, cucumbers have prickles on them. You've got to be careful."

"You think?" I smart back as I drop my bucket and start toward the house. I'm done.

"Come back here young lady," she hollers. As much as I want to go in the air-conditioned house I know I can't disrespect her right now. I know that's my key to getting off this farm. Taking a deep breath, I stop, face her, and carefully inspect each cucumber before I pick it. When Gran has punished me long enough she tells me that she's almost finished so I can go inside. I hurry inside, scrub my hands, and make myself a sandwich.

After lunch I hide out in my room with my music on loud and focus on my flexibility. I've got to do something. I can already feel the resistance in my muscles from lack of daily practice. What's going to happen in another month? Realizing I have no room in here, I decide to brave the humidity and heat while I try to find myself in the music.

BARRICK

Ms. Mae comes to visit me as I'm finishing up for the day. She informs me that she is lightening up on Cadence. She will still report to me every morning and help, but her duties will be done before lunch. I kind of hate it. It's been fun watching her squirm and get out of her comfort zone. Not to mention, she's a lot prettier to look at than the cows.

After cleaning the equipment, I make sure that all of the tubs of water are full for all of the animals. The heat is brutal this time of year. As I am placing the water hose back on the rack, I hear the craziest music coming from the house. I close the gate and peer out the door. I'm completely caught off guard when I see Cadence moving to that awful music. She has on shorts that barely cover her bottom and a sports bra. Her sunshine blond hair is pulled up perfectly, and as I watch her movements, her body is doing things I've never seen anyone do in my life. The music changes from raw to classical. As I continue to watch I'm blown away at her flexibility. *Dang, if she can stretch like that then I wonder...* that thought is quickly eliminated when I realize I shouldn't be having those thoughts about Cadence.

I quickly walk toward my truck trying to get her image out of my mind. As I flip the ignition, I jump out of my seat as heavy metal music blares through my speakers at the highest volume. I spin the knob down and hit preset number one for my favorite station. Pausing, to settle myself I realize that Cadence just got me back for the compost pile. Well, bring it on city girl.

CADENCE

As the music plays, I stretch, listen to the beat, and fall in rhythm. I try to focus on the routine, but something's not right. I move with more emotion, but when I glance over my shoulder, I realize what's missing... Lauren. This piece was picked to show off both of our assets. She always had such grace when moving while I could build a fire beneath my feet. The anger and chaos always fueled my creativity. It's like she was the light while I was the darkness, and together we made a complete day. Feeling defeated, I turn off the music and pause. I will not let living in this place stop me from dancing. If I can't go home, there has to be a way for me to find myself without her, but I refuse to go to some hillbilly studio. I am alone with no partner, friends, or even a dad for that matter. For now, I'll just dance on the farm until I can find out when the recruiters will be in the big city. I push the anger down deep inside and dance for me. I hit shuffle on my playlist and focus on my poise and movements with each song. When "Talk Dirty To Me" begins to play I laugh and move to the music.

"What in tarnation is that?" I hear Gran yell as the screen door slams behind her.

"Jason Derulo, Gran," I say as I mute the music.

"Girl, that was not music. I know exactly where we're going Saturday night. The Loft. You need to hear some good country music."

"Gran, I hate country music."

"Well, that's what's wrong with ya. Everyone needs some Cash, Straight, or Luke Bryan in their life," she says with a laugh. "But seriously sweetie, you were so graceful before that other Jason Julio came on."

"You mean Derulo, Gran."

Tossing her hands in the air she walks back into the house, "After watching that maybe I should take you to that studio."

I laugh at the thought of joining a studio here. I mean, what could they possibly teach me that I don't already know?

"Everything okay?" I'm startled by Mom's voice.

"Yeah, just trying to think about what I want to do with this routine."

"Okay. Well, Gran wanted to show you around town tonight. Didn't know if you wanted to shower first," she says.

I look at her like she's lost her mind because I might be in Delight, North Carolina, but this city girl doesn't go anywhere without looking like a million bucks.

"Hurry up," she says as I make my way toward my room. I know exactly what I'm wearing. I go to my closet and choose my pale pink shorts and my sheer Elie Tahari sleeveless blouse. I take a shower, shave, style my hair, and apply my makeup with ease. Popping my lips one last time, I smile knowing that you can take the girl out of the city, but you cannot take the city out of the girl.

As my heels click on the steps, Gran and Mom look at me. Gran shakes her head, and looks at Mom. "Mama, she's not going to change who she is because we moved south."

"Well, a Gran can hope. That's for sure," she says with a laugh.

Walking outside we get into Gran's beat-up truck and I sit on my hands in hopes of not getting my shorts dirty. She rolls down the windows and begins to drive us around the farm. I look at the dash for the air conditioner button, but there's nothing there. You've got to be kidding, at least Barrick's truck had everything you could imagine. I try to figure out how I'm going to refrain from sweating, but within a few minutes the first bubble skims my skin. She points out the animals, crops, and tells us a story about everything. *Can she not be quiet for two seconds?*

We spend the next hour driving around Delight and Lawndale. I'm thankful she's reached sixty miles an hour. It's not cold air, but at least it's something. She points out who lives where, who owns what, the church, school, The Loft, and areas of town that are off limits. By the time we arrive back at her house, I'm sweating like crazy, my makeup is melted off, and my shorts are wet and have a streak of red dirt on them. *You've got to be kidding!*

As soon as we are back at the house, my brain is on overload, and my pores are crying. I'm seriously going to have to figure out a way to keep up my appearance with this heat but right now, the only thing on my mind is another shower.

13

BARRICK

I've been watching Cadence dance every afternoon this week. I'm amazed at her grace, anger, poise, and attitude. It doesn't matter the song, she changes with the beat of the music. I'm surprised I haven't gotten caught yet but I enjoy watching the real Cadence. I've seen plenty of dancers but none that can show their true feelings with their movements like she can. Her determination and drive amaze me as she practices outside in the heat of the day. Today is Thursday and Cadence and I have to work the farmers' market again. As I load my truck with milk, eggs, and produce, I realize I'm disappointed that this will be the last one we work together with school starting next week.

The market is busy and we work in silence side by side. We quickly sell out and are relieved we get to leave before it gets too hot. I try to talk Cadence into stopping for lunch but she refuses. I don't know what her deal is. One minute she's hot and the next she's cold as ice. I swear, girls! They make no sense at all especially ones that are from above the Mason-Dixon line.

Arriving back at the farm, she excuses herself and I begin to place the buckets from the market back in the storage room when I notice that there is a hissing sound coming from the other side of the barn. As I go to check it out, it doesn't take long to realize that the Gator tire has sprung a leak. Great! Ms. Mae uses this all the time. Why couldn't this have happened before we drove to town? Luckily for me, there's a John Deere store in Lawndale. Yes, I know it sounds insane. We don't have a McDonald's but we have a John Deere. I quickly crank up my truck and head to the store for a new tire.

When I arrive back at the farm, I notice that Ms. Mae is sitting on the front porch, but Cadence isn't anywhere to be seen, which is odd. She is usually dancing out in the sun right about now. I kill the engine and open my door. That's when I hear music coming from the barn. Grabbing the tire, I walk toward the barn and the music grows louder the closer I get. When I open the door, the music attacks me. Cadence is at the opposite end of the barn that faces the pasture. The tire makes a loud thud as I drop it on the ground beside the Gator, but the noise doesn't faze her. I prop myself up against a beam and watch; I feel like I'm intruding on something extremely personal. As the song ends and there is a lapse between the next one, I feel that I have to let her know that I'm here. "You think you can teach me a few of those moves?" I ask with a smile that quickly fades when she jumps out of her skin.

"How long have you been standing there?" she questions as she grabs her music and hits pause.

"Long enough," I say as I push off the beam and close the distance between us.

As I'm within an arm's reach of her, she can't seem to get her thoughts together, which is weird since she's usually quick-witted. "You know that's rude. Watching someone without them knowing. What are you, a stalker?" she asks in a harsh tone with her arms crossed, which tells me not to come a step closer.

"No Cadence, I'm not a stalker, believe me. What are you doing out here anyways? Don't you normally tutu around in the yard?" I say as I point toward the house.

She gasps. "So you *have* been watching me. I can't believe you! I just want to have some time to myself, and I don't need someone watching me."

"Well, for what it's worth, you're incredible," I say and mean every word. I've never seen anything like that in my life, and I know more about dance than any country boy should *ever* know.

"What? What do you know about dance? I was half a second behind the beat and my toes weren't pointed enough," she says as she moves her hands to her hips.

"Oh, I know more than you think I do. You're amazing. I've never seen anything like it in my life. You really should find somewhere to do that, ya know, in the air conditioning." I smirk.

"Gran says there's some studio down the road. There is no way it can compare to my studio in New York. I'm sure that I can dance circles around those country bumpkins," she mouths off.

I shake my head as she grabs her music and storms past me. There's no need to try and argue with her or even try to make a point. I've learned watching my parents. The woman is always right... no matter if they are dead wrong.

CADENCE

I don't know who he thinks he is standing in there watching me like that. Who does that? Not to mention trying to tell me I should go to a studio. What does he know about dance? I bet he has white boy moves where he barely sways to the music. I laugh at my mental picture of Barrick attempting to dance.

As I enter the house, I don't see anyone. I talk to myself as I stomp toward my room. Pacing the floor back and forth, I begin to talk out loud and answer myself when there is a knock at my door.

"Cade, everything okay?" Gran asks.

"No! That boy out there was watching me dance," I say pointing toward the barn. Gran begins to laugh and that makes me madder. "It's not funny," I say as tears form in my eyes from my anger.

She tries to stop laughing but takes a second. "I believe you're talking about Barrick. You've met him before, worked with him, and I believe even pranked him. You've seen him every day since you arrived. I don't know why you are so mad."

"Gran, he was all propped up in the barn staring at me. He didn't even bother to get my attention. Who does that?"

"Maybe he liked what he saw," she says as she lifts her eyebrows several times.

"Ugh! Gran! You really think I want a guy in my life right now? I've got more things to worry about."

"Lawd child. I didn't mean it like that, but he is pretty to look at if I say so myself. I meant you've been here almost two weeks and haven't met anyone your age."

"Well, whose fault is that?" I seethe at her.

"Missy, don't start that with me. You're the one that was disrespectful and needed to learn a thing or two. I thought we were making progress, but maybe I was wrong."

I pause and look at her. "What do you mean?"

"I meant that I called the studio to find out about classes, but I can easily hold out on that information if needed. You are to respect everyone 'round here whether you like them or not. Do you understand?" she asks with her arms crossed.

"That's out. I don't need a friend and surely not a guy."

She pauses as concern flashes across her face, and I know what is coming next. "Tell me what this is really about."

"Nothing Gran. It's fine. I'll be just fine." *Fine. Isn't that the word we all use to try and sugarcoat life? My life is fine. It was fine when my dad left and it's fine now that I'm stuck on this farm. Just fine.*

"Well, we all know what fine means so if you aren't going to talk to me, I suggest you either do as I say and be nice or I'll find you something to do inside to pass the time. School starts in four days, and you've still got a lot to learn before then."

"What do I need to do inside?" I ask because I do *not* want to see Barrick.

"For starters, go down to the basement and grab two boxes of canning jars. We've got tomatoes to can and salsa to make."

I walk past her, down the hall, and toward the basement. I've never been down here before. Turning on the light attached to a pull string, I see wall space lined with canned goods. Who eats all of this? I glance at them and then walk to the end of the steps. Looking around, I have no idea where they might be so I glance in several boxes until I find them.

"Cadence, did you find them?" Gran yells down the steps.

"Yeah. I'm coming," I say as I take one box and then return for the other. Gran and I spend the remainder of the day washing the jars and cooking the tomatoes to make spaghetti sauce and dicing them for salsa. By the time Mom gets home from work, I'm sick and tired of looking at them and smelling like them, but we aren't finished.

After the last batch is complete, Gran pulls together a dinner using the fresh salsa. It's beyond amazing.

"Gran, this is great! It's way better than Mi Pueblo."

"Of course it is, and the longer it sits, the hotter it gets," she says as she does a cha-cha move. I shake my head.

After dinner, I look at the kitchen and it's a disaster. Without being told, I begin to clean up. Gran thanks me and tells me that if I'm not going to help Barrick then I will be helping her in the house canning the next two days. Tomorrow's agenda is corn. Just lovely.

BARRICK

After the long day I had, I'm exhausted when I get home. My parents are home and Mom has supper ready, but my sister isn't home yet. I swear that girl will come running in here at the last second. We eat supper together every night and she knows she'll be in trouble if she's late. Checking my watch, I know that I have a little bit of time before she gets home so I decide to go ahead and shower.

After supper, Dad calls me into the living room to discuss classes. He's taken it upon himself to register me at the local community college. I'm not thrilled, but I know in the long run it will be worth it. My dad is a good 'ole country boy. He's gone each morning before we are awake to make sure he's home by supper unless there's something catastrophic. We've got a small farm, a few animals and garden. It's enough for us to use but not make a profit like Ms. Mae. I know that I want to work on a farm, have my own to be exact, and I want to make a profit. I guess a few business classes won't hurt.

14

CADENCE

*F*riday and Saturday morning I'm greeted by endless trailers full of corn. Gran takes a few moments to show me how to do it correctly, and it doesn't seem like a big deal. I pull the husks back, as she calls them, and toss them into a bucket then I take a brush to remove the excess silks. *Wonder why they call them silks?* I continue to follow Gran's directions as Barrick takes a seat and begins to help as well.

I begin to feel confident with a task on the farm for the first time since I've arrived. Gran excuses herself and I'm left with him.

"So I take it you're finished with the cows?" he asks.

"Yeah. I've been helping Gran inside."

"Look, I'm sorry—"

"Get it Barrick! Get it!" I squeal as I jump out of my chair and drop the ear of corn.

He stands to see what's going on and Gran walks briskly toward me. Barrick leans down and picks it up and starts to laugh.

"It's just a worm," he says as he places it on his finger and brings it toward me.

"Gran! Make him stop!" She begins to laugh.

"Why am I always the butt of all these jokes?" They both pause and look at each other. "I don't do cows, snakes, poop, bugs, spiders, or worms. Got it!" I say as I begin to walk off.

Barrick grabs my wrist. "Hold up. I was just messin' with ya."

"Yeah you seem to do a lot of that," I smart back.

"You two knock it off. We've got more where this comes from. Cadence why don't you silk and I'll shuck."

"Fine," I say as I take a seat.

When the trailer is almost empty, Barrick heads to the field to pick more as we take the ears in to wash, place in bags, date them, and place in the freezer.

As we finish, he arrives with another trailer load. *Why aren't we finished yet?* I soon realize this isn't something we are going to finish today. It's not like a few ears, it's like an entire field of corn. *How in the world can this much grow on Gran's farm?* Every time I think we're almost done another trailer arrives with a new load to shuck.

When the phone rings, Gran excuses herself, and I'm left with Barrick. We sit in silence for several minutes.

Placing an ear of corn in the bucket, my eyes meet his.

"Look, earlier I was trying to tell you I'm sorry about intruding on you the other day. I won't do it again, but for the record, I did try to get your attention."

"Next time try harder," I say as I continue to silk the corn.

We sit in silence until Gran comes out of the house holding some huge rectangle. *What in the world?* Barrick stands to help her.

"I figured we needed a break. I'll be right back with some tea," she says as she goes back in the house.

She hands Barrick a glass, and then hands me one that she swears has hardly any sugar. I take a sip and I can see that she made an effort even though she only diluted it with water instead of actually making it with less sugar. As she sits, she turns a switch on the rectangle thingy and country music fills the air. *Ah, an old-fashioned radio.* I take a deep breath because it's hot, a worm attacked me, and I have to listen to this awful racket.

Gran doesn't say anything, she just takes a sip of her tea and places it on the ground before standing and beginning to dance around. When I notice Barrick's head is moving to the beat of the music, I don't know if I can take it anymore. I stand and begin to walk toward the house.

"Cadence, you too good for Gran's music?" she asks as she does an old lady dance move.

"Nah, but that is terrible," I say as Barrick shakes his head. "What are you thinking country boy?"

"Girl, you wouldn't stand a chance at The Loft."

Gran starts to laugh. "Why's that so funny, Gran?"

"'Cause that's all they play." As I start to comment, Gran begins to bounce up and down, and I'm extremely worried about her.

"Gran! Are you okay?" I question with concern.

"Cade! This is my jam!" Oh my, Gran should *never* use that terminology. "This is how we roll!" She begins to sing and I'm so embarrassed for her. I look at Barrick to see if we should stop her, but then I see him singing and bobbing his head to the beat. I take my hands and cover my face from the horror.

"Gran! Oh my gosh! Stop! Pleeeeease!" I say as I begin to laugh.

As the song fades, she looks in my direction. "I don't care what your mama and daddy say, your dancin' skills came from your Gran." I sit there speechless as she attempts to do some dancing jig. "Cadence, that's Florida Georgia Line. You need to listen to them. Isn't that right, Barrick?"

"Yes, Ms. Mae. Florida Georgia Line is pretty awesome," he says with a smile.

"I think I need to take Cadence to The Loft tomorrow, watcha think Barrick?" she asks looking at him, but he doesn't reply.

"Ms. Mae. I don't know if she's ready for that," he says as he walks toward the tractor for another load of corn.

BARRICK

I had to get out of there. There is no way that Cadence will survive a night at The Loft. The food is amazing, but the teen crowd can be brutal to outsiders. I'm going to say a prayer for Cadence that Ms. Mae changes her mind.

After a long afternoon of cleaning corn, we call it a day. I promise to help tomorrow morning so that we can finish by lunch.

When I walk in the barn for the morning milking I'm surprised to see an older version of Cadence already working with the cattle.

"Hi! Hope you don't mind. Just figured I could help out. I'm Regina," she says as she extends her hand.

"Barrick," I say as I meet hers.

"Yeah, I've heard," she says with a smile, and I know exactly where Cadence gets her looks. "I've almost finished. If you'll help me clean up, we can go in and eat breakfast before we start on the corn."

I work alongside her and she is so polite. She's the exact opposite of Cadence. When we're just about done, I tell her I can finish up and she heads for the house.

As I approach the steps, I can smell the bacon in the air and my stomach begins to growl. I give a polite knock before I walk in. I'm thoroughly impressed to see that Cadence isn't drinking a green shake, but instead has eggs, or egg whites at least, and a piece of toast. *That girl's got to live a little.* I also notice that she is dressed like she's going out. Doesn't she remember we're shucking corn again today? Ms. Mae piles my plate high, and I take the only open seat, which is beside Cadence.

After we eat, I wash my plate and begin to help clean the kitchen when Ms. Mae excuses me to go ahead and bring the trailer. She informs Cadence that she will finish it, and of course, right on cue Cadence rolls her eyes.

We work quickly and even have great conversation, except for Cadence. She keeps checking her cellphone and doesn't find anything amusing. Her mother is a hoot. You can see that she enjoys being back here.

"Barrick, I think I'm gonna take them to The Loft tonight. I think it would be good for both of them. Plus, I'm ready to shake a leg," Ms. Mae states as she continues to shuck the corn.

"Ummmm." I stumble for the words, then Regina comments.

"As in the dance hall, Mama?" she questions.

"That's the one! Cadence here had some garbage on her music box the other day and she doesn't know who... gosh what are their names?"

"Florida Georgia Line." I throw in to help her out.

"That's it! She needs an education, and school starts Monday. She needs to know what to expect."

Regina looks up from her ear of corn, "So you think taking her to the local honky-tonk is going to help?"

"Yup! It will help you too. You know you always loved that place growing up," Ms. Mae says with a wink.

"Mama! I was a stupid teenager."

"See that's what I'm talkin' 'bout. Both of you need a good dose of country living. Regina, you decided to go to the haughty school in New York and thought you were too good. Bless Cadence's heart, it's rubbed off on her. We're good folks 'round here and don't both of you forget it."

On that note, I excuse myself and grab the last trailer of corn.

15

CADENCE

*H*oly crap. Gran is going to make us go to that hillbilly two-step place tonight. Just awesome! I can't wait to finish so I can call Lauren and tell her how exciting my life has become.

Barrick leaves after he finishes shucking and taking care of the cows once more. Mom and I have to continue to clean the corn for the remainder of the afternoon. I swear it's like Bubba on *Forrest Gump* with all those types of shrimp. I've see corn on the cob, off the cob, creamed corn, and made corn relish. Who knew there were so many ways to prepare corn? I thought you took it out of a can.

As soon as I'm excused, I hurry to my room, close the door, and call Lauren.

"Hello?"

"Hey girl!" Lauren squeals. "What's going on?"

"Oh, nothing except being elbows deep in corn and hardly getting any time for myself."

"Grouchy much?" Lauren states with a hint of sarcasm.

"You would be too. I'm stuck out here in the middle of nowhere.

It's hot and sticky. I ruined my favorite pair of shorts. I drink milk straight out of a cow tit and to top it all off, I caught Mr. Farmhand watching me dance."

"How old is he? Is he hot? Did you get that picture yet? Please tell me he looks like Scott Eastwood in, what was that movie?"

"Don't know, don't care, no, and *The Longest Ride*."

"Why don't you move in with me?"

"Lauren, we've already tried that. Mom vetoed that quickly. I wish you could come visit here at least."

"Well after that fabulous endorsement, it sounds like so much fun," she says sarcastically. "So tell me, what's really bothering you?"

"Well, I haven't left Gran's except for a tour of the town and the only person I know is Barrick, who drives me insane and really seems to want to stick it to me. Gran is being a hard-ass and won't take me to the dance studio and Mom won't stick up for me and school starts next week. On top of all that, they want to take me to some dance hall and subject me to country music. I mean it's like they don't even care what I want or about the stuff I like. I mean country music? All that whining and sad stuff? It's not my fault we're here so why do I have to accept all their crap? They'll probably want me to dance with some guy with no teeth!"

She starts to laugh and I laugh with her. It feels good. "I miss you, Lauren."

"Same here, girl. My solo just isn't the same as when we worked together. On a lighter note, what are you going to wear to a country dance hall? A tutu? Ballet shoes? Oh I got it! How about a tutu and cowboy boots?" she suggests and starts laughing.

"Oh that would be a sight, I'm sure! I'm just going to be me, but there's no way in I'm dancing."

"Oh, I bet they are going to have some of those line dances. Oh my gosh, they are awful. Can't they do any real dancing? Well, I've got to go. Call me tomorrow and tell me all about it."

"You know I will. Love ya, girl." We disconnect and I feel like a little hole that's been missing in my heart has been filled.

Placing my phone on my bed, I begin to contemplate what I'm

going to wear. I want to be me, and that's exactly what I plan on doing. I open my closet door, look down at my bubblegum pink Giuseppe Zanotti sandals, and know exactly what I'm wearing.

I take a shower and take my time getting ready. After curling my hair and pinning it in place, I take out my Vionnet paint-splattered crop-top-and-short set. It's sassy, stands out, and accents all of my assets perfectly. If I'm going to make a first impression in this town, it's going to be one that lasts. I slide on my sandals and buckle them in place as I hear Mom call for me to hurry up.

Grabbing my matching clutch, I glance in the mirror one more time and hurry to the stairs. Barrick is at the bottom talking to Gran. *I thought he went home already.* He stops mid-sentence and meets my eyes while my good mood quickly fades.

"Hey Cadence, looks like you're ready for a night out on the town but I'm not sure you're ready for The Loft," he says.

I just smirk and walk into the kitchen where my mom is waiting.

As soon as the door is shut, Gran is on my case. "You listen to me missy! You might not be from 'round here, but in my house we are respectful. That was not respect. So drop the attitude. I will not tolerate it. Do you understand?"

"Yeah," I huff.

"Excuse me?" she says, looking at Mom. "I know my daughter didn't raise a girl to be rude to others."

"No ma'am, I didn't," Mom says like she's a child being scolded. "Cadence, that's enough. I'm not sure what your deal is, but drop it," she says as her eyes plead for me to play nice.

"Really? You don't? You took me away from my friends, my home, and the stuff I love and you don't know what's wrong with me? How about being in the middle of nowhere working next to a guy that seems to want to stick it to me? How about not having any friends here and school is about to start?"

"Cadence, I understand you are upset but you should still be respectful."

Gran doesn't say a word and heads to the door.

I toss my arms to my side, let out a deep breath, and walk down the steps. Let's get this over with already.

Thankfully Gran lets Mom drive the Suburban. I wasn't looking forward to ruining another outfit. The ride to The Loft isn't too long, but my mind is reeling from what just happened and I have no idea what to expect at this Loft place. The one thing I'm positive of is that Barrick will not be there tonight. He was just heading home in worn out jeans and a shirt and couldn't possibly be ready for a night out.

Arriving at The Loft, I notice it looks completely different than when we drove past the other day. The parking lot is full of cars and it's well lit. Once Mom puts the Suburban in park, Gran grabs her arm.

"Let's have a good time tonight. What do you say?" she says to Mom and then looks at me. Mom agrees and I plaster a fake smile on my face.

Entering the doorway, I take in my surroundings. No farm life – that's a plus. Beautiful, detailed beams running above the dance floor with strings of lights attached to them – another plus. It almost looks like something out of a movie and I think it might actually not be that bad. That thought is dashed when a lady, who doesn't speak proper English, asks us 'how many' while smacking her gum loudly. She's even wearing a plaid shirt and boots. Ugh! She needs a serious lesson in fashion. I glance at Mom who smirks, and must be thinking exactly the same as me.

Gran tells her how many, and she leads us to a table with a view of the dance floor. There isn't anyone on it, but country music is playing in the background. Lord, help me. The hostess tells us the specials. I look at the menu and figure I'm safe with a salad. When I place my order I swear Gran rolls her eyes.

We sit and talk about what has been going on. Mom talks about her job, and as much as I hate that it's not as glamorous as her job in New York, she does seem happy. Mom asks if I'm ready to start school on Monday and if I have everything I need. Of course I'm ready. I don't have a choice. I only need a few school supplies but what's there to stress about?

Gran chimes in our conversation. "I thought we could go check out the studio on Monday. If you like it, you could go a few days a week after school. What do you think?"

"Gran, why can't I go to a big city like Charlotte or something?" I question.

"Because the studio in town is best of the best from what I understand. You should give it a try."

"I think I'll pass for now."

Mom looks at me. "I thought that's what you wanted, Cadence?"

"I want to dance somewhere with prestige and there's no way that is it. I'm better off dancing in the backyard at Gran's."

"Heavens to Betsy, girl! You've got to get over yourself."

We finish eating and pay for our food. I'm impressed to see Mom drink a beer straight from the bottle. I think I've only ever seen her drink wine in a glass.

"Come on, the band will be starting soon," Gran says with excitement. What happened to a DJ? We move from our table, to one closer to the dance floor and wait for the band to begin playing. With the first pull on the fiddle, my ears feel like they are being attacked. As the music gets louder so do the people, and before long the dance floor is covered in people attempting to dance. I notice a few groups of girls my age. They are in frayed, cut-off jeans, tank tops, and boots. Seriously, that's the style here? After people watching for as long as I can stand, I excuse myself to go to the restroom, but I'm not prepared for the looks I get as I make my way there. Every eye is on me. I smile, sway my hips a little harder, and hold my head high. I said I was going to let them know Cadence Lewis had arrived, and I've succeeded. Bring on Monday!

———

BARRICK

After arriving at The Loft, I stand outside and talk to my buddies for a little bit until the band begins to play. When we hear the music start,

we make our way inside and stand near the bar. As I scan the crowd, I
see Cadence sitting with Ms. Mae and Regina. Man, she looks hot and
I was right, she doesn't fit in at The Loft. I can't imagine what
everyone will think of her. I hope they show her a little southern
hospitality because let's face it, her attitude isn't exactly sweet.

I watch her and am pulled from my thought by one of my boys.

"Who you staring at?" Aaron questions.

"No one. Just tired's all," I say playing it off, but at that exact
moment, she stands. I wait to see how long it takes for people to
notice her. As she walks across the dance floor toward the restroom,
all eyes are on her. I do my best not to stare, but she's making it
almost impossible in those heels and short shorts. I've never seen
anything like that and neither has this town.

"Who's that?" he asks.

"Ms. Mae's granddaughter."

"You're kidding right?" I shake my head no. "Where's she been
hiding all these years?" He smiles.

"NewYork."

"Well when she gets back, this country boy is going to show her a
good time," he says as he rubs his hands together like he's about to win
the lottery. I don't say anything. Deep down I want to tell him he
doesn't have a chance but, where's the fun in that? I'd rather stand
back and watch.

Within a few minutes Cadence has returned to her table. Ms. Mae
gets asked to dance by an older gentleman and her mom gets asked by
Hamilton Parks. Aaron smiles at me as he makes his way to Cadence. I
prop my arm on the bar and watch the scene that's about to go down.

CADENCE

Oh crap! Mom and Gran have left me alone to dance with these hillbillies and now I'm under attack. I put on a smile that's laced with
venom.

"Well, hello ma'am," he says as he takes a step toward me. I smile yet again. "I'm Aaron. What's a pretty lady like yourself doing all alone?" Oh. My. God. Please tell me this doesn't work on girls around here.

"For starters, I'm not a ma'am. Don't ever call me that again, and I'm just hanging out waiting on those two," I say trying to show a lack of interest as I point toward Mom and Gran.

"Would you like to dance?" he asks as he places his hand out for mine. I look at it, and politely tell him no. He looks as if I just stole his puppy, and I laugh to myself. I said I'd come here tonight, but I promised myself I wouldn't dance to this awful music. That is one promise I'm keeping. He takes my no in defeat and moves on to the group of girls I saw earlier. One with long, dark hair smiles from ear to ear and follows him to the dance floor.

After a few songs Mom and Gran join me, and then everyone in the place gets on their feet to participate in a line dance. *Who is this lady I call Mom and what has Delight done to her?*

I look in their direction and point toward the door. I grab Mom's keys, and decide that I need some peace and quiet. I take a seat in the Suburban. Rolling down my windows, I realize it's not as sticky as earlier today and there is a slight breeze. It feels good. I take my phone and check social media, text Lauren, and see that Dad has yet to contact me.

As I'm thinking about school, I hear a group of people talking and I eavesdrop on their conversation. It's the girls, as well as a few guys, from earlier and they are talking about me. Are you freaking kidding me? Then suddenly I hear his voice.

"Maddie, can't you give the girl a break?" Barrick asks.

"What's your deal, Barrick? You like her or something?" She laughs and the other girls follow suit.

"Shut up. You don't know her," he says defensively. I take my hand and place it on the door handle and debate whether to say something or not. I decide I need to say a few choice words so they know who they are dealing with.

Flinging the door open, I make my way to the other side of the truck. "So Maddie is it? Seems you have a lot to say about the new girl, care to say any of it to my face?" I ask with my arms crossed. She looks like she's seen a ghost as her mouth hits the floor. "That's what I thought. I'm Cadence by the way. That way you don't have to call me *that girl who's not from 'round here',*" I say with a country accent before smiling at Barrick and walking back to our vehicle.

16

BARRICK

She smiled. She freaking smiled at me and it wasn't a fake one either. That's got to be a step in the right direction, but then again I might need to be extra cautious when I crank my truck Monday. I turn back to the group and tell my sister it's time to go. She tells me to hold on, and I tell her I'll meet her at the truck. I don't know why she wants to hang out with Maddie anyway. She's that way since I can remember.

Sitting in my truck, I can't quit thinking about Cadence. The way she didn't care what others thought, the attitude she put on display, and the way she shot Aaron down without a thought. There's a reason she's this way, and I plan on figuring it out one way or the other.

Twenty minutes later my sister gets in the truck and just looks at me for a minute. "What was your deal back there?"

"Nothin'. I just don't get why you insist on hanging out with Maddie."

"I know Barrick, but she's one of those people who makes your life hard if you aren't on her side."

"So you mean to tell me you'd rather be one of those mean girls than be who you are?"

"No. I just don't know where I fit in."

"Just be you. I like you just like you are."

She rolls her eyes. *What is it with girls and rolling their eyes?* "You have to like me. You're my brother."

Our ride home doesn't take long, and I stop my sister before we go in the house. "Look, Cadence is different, and I really think you need to give her a shot Monday."

"I will. You know I'm not like Maddie, and I believe everyone deserves a fair shot. Thanks for waiting on me tonight."

"Did you really think that I was gonna leave my little sister?"

"Oh my gosh, we're the same freakin' age right now Barrick," she says with an eye roll.

That night I lie in bed and replay the events of the night, and when I can't sleep I decide to do a little digging. I open my social media and search for Cadence Lewis. I look at her pictures and her friends. It's obvious that Cadence comes from a world that I know nothing about. She has pictures of her dancing, her friends, and her family. I notice that she is always perfectly dressed and she's continued to do that here as well. Scrolling back through the pictures I notice a nice-looking gentleman always in a suit or dress shirt. His hair is combed back and he's in several pictures with Cadence and her mom. They look so happy, but all of a sudden he's missing. I can't help but wonder if that has something to do with Cadence's current attitude.

CADENCE

I'm pissed on the entire ride home. I've texted Lauren the entire way and I feel my blood pressure rising. Who tdoes that Maddie girl think she is? I know this little spat is just the beginning. I better get my game face on for Monday.

I try my best to go to sleep, but it's impossible. I toss my covers off, put on some dance clothes and grab my ear buds and iPod. I flip on the porch light and strap my iPod to my arm and get lost in the music. When my limbs are numb and I can't keep my eyes open, I walk to my room, where I fall onto the bed with the music still playing.

CADENCE

*T*he next morning Gran comes in my room and tells me to get my lazy self up and get ready for church. Um, no, not going. Within ten minutes, Mom comes in and says the same thing. I'm not saying I'm against church, I just know that today, I'm not going. I'm exhausted and tomorrow is the first day of school. They leave me in bed, and I sleep until they return.

Lunch on Sundays is unique at Gran's. She looks like she's cooked a Thanksgiving feast. What's the deal with that? My stomach growls as I make my plate. Gran laughs and tells me I better eat more than just a vegetable or two. I have to agree that missing breakfast and only having a salad last night has made my stomach an angry organ and I believe it's ready to attack me.

Mom, Gran, and I sit and talk while we eat. Gran informs me that I can drive her truck to school tomorrow or for as long as I like. She said with Barrick here during the day, she's got transportation if she needs it, but she swears she only needs the Gator.

"Um, Gran. I'm not driving that truck. It will probably break down on me, and I'll be lost in the middle of nowhere. Besides do you know how long it's been since I drove an actual car?" She looks at me confused. "Gran, I don't know how to get there and I haven't driven in months."

She shakes her head. "Cadence, turn right out of the driveway, and turn right at the stoplight in Lawndale. It's down the road on the right. You can't miss it. It's not a big deal."

Mom chimes in. "Cadence, you don't have a choice, honey. That's your only option."

"Fine, but I've got to clean it out or something."

They both look at each other and shrug their shoulders. After lunch, I decide to pick out my outfit for tomorrow, and then clean out Gran's truck. I'm shocked when I step outside and see Barrick's truck at the barn. Doesn't he ever take a day off? I shake my head and walk toward the truck.

As I pull the rusted handle, I say very ugly words in my head toward Gran and Mom for making me drive this piece of junk. I clear out the trash, and then use a wet towel to clean the seats. When I finally feel that the seats will not stain my name brand clothes tomorrow, I climb in to get comfortable. Honestly, I can't remember the last time I drove. You never have to drive in the city.

There isn't any power anything. I try to move the seat back for my long legs, but get angry as I pull the lever and it doesn't move. When it finally does, it slides back too far. I hit my hand on the steering wheel. As I look to my right, I burst out laughing from agitation. There's no way I can drive this truck. It's not an automatic.

I get out of the truck, slam the door, and march myself to the house. "Gran, you've got to take me. I can't drive that truck," I say as I point toward it.

"What do you mean?" she questions.

"I can only drive an automatic. Please! There's no way I can drive that truck."

Gran stands and walks to the truck. "Cadence, you're going to learn how to drive this truck. Get in," she says while holding the driver's side door open.

Gran then walks around and gets in the passenger seat. "For starters, take a deep breath. It won't do ya any good to try and learn worked up like that." I look at her like she's lost her mind. I exhale slowly. "Push the clutch in and put the truck in second." I do as she says. "Now, let up on the clutch and press the gas at the same time." I do as she says and the truck moves and jerks like it's having a seizure before the engine dies.

"Great! I broke it!" I say with my arms crossed.

"You didn't break it. You just let out the clutch too fast. Come on Cadence. Let's try it again." Gran attempts to teach me for the next thirty minutes. We spend most of that time with her yelling and me yelling back. She tells me to get out of the truck and I can walk to school tomorrow.

"Grrrrrrrr!" I yell as she walks into the house. So much for her having patience. I'm so screwed.

Barrick

I try my best not to watch Ms. Mae and Cadence, but let's face it, it's free entertainment. I finish giving the animals water and that's when I hear Ms. Mae yell at her. Dang. I don't think I've ever heard her like that. I shake my head, but then I hear Cadence yell as well. *Should I check on her or not?* I debate for a few minutes, and decide I might as well. If she starts throwing something at me, I'll retreat.

Walking to the other side of the barn, I see her walking in circles talking with her hands. I stop to think this through. *Do I really want to do this?* I look around and go for it.

"Um, you know what they say about people who talk to themselves," I say while making a crazy sign by my head as she snaps her head my direction.

"I feel about freaking crazy."

"You want me to help ya?" I ask, motioning toward the truck.

"It's hopeless," she states.

"Nah. Come on." I tell her to get in the passenger side. "Listen to the engine and watch what my feet do." She looks at me like she doesn't understand. "How do you find the beat of the music?" I question.

"I feel it."

"Exactly. This works the same way. You've got to feel it." We spend the next ten minutes riding around as she watches what I do. I pull into the school parking lot and tell her it's her turn. "You got this," I say as I open the driver's side door and wait for her to walk around. I help her move the seat to her perfect setting.

Walking around, I sit in the passenger seat and say a little prayer that I made sense because if not, I'm about to have a serious case of whiplash.

She takes a deep breath and lifts her foot from the clutch but doesn't press the gas. I can see the irritation flare. She does it again. The engine dies again. After four unsuccessful attempts, she gets the truck moving and I can see the excitement on her face. It quickly fades as she forgets to switch gears.

When the engine dies, she throws her hands up in defeat. "Look, you got excited. You got it this time. I'll help ya." As the engine comes to life, she finds a happy medium between the gas and clutch and begins to move. When the engine is approaching a transition, I tell her and she's driving in circles around the parking lot in no time with a smile on her face.

"You ready to try the road?" I question.

"Yeah," she says and we turn to make our way back to the farm with only one stall out.

Ms. Mae and Regina are on the porch talking when we get back. They pause when they see the truck approaching. Cadence puts it in park and almost forgets to press the emergency break, but as it starts to roll she remembers.

"See it wasn't that bad," I tell her.

"If you say so. Let's see if I can do this tomorrow on the way to school." I can't help but laugh at the fact that Cadence and her prissy self has to drive Ms. Mae's old beat-up truck. "What are you going to do about your classes? Is this your last day around here?" she questions.

"Nah, actually, I scheduled my classes at the community college to work around my schedule here."

"Oh," she says and I can't help but wonder why she asked.

18

CADENCE

*a*s my alarm rings on Monday morning, I toss the covers off and am ready to take on the day. I've got to take my time getting ready this morning. First impressions are important, and last night I chose the perfect outfit. I slide on my nude-colored Brazil dairy shell skirt paired with a white blouse and laced-up stilettos.

Grabbing my white handbag and just enough school supplies to get through the first day, I walk to the kitchen to pour myself a cup of coffee. Gran is sitting at the kitchen table and Mom is gathering her things for work.

"Mom, you sure you can't drop me off?" I question because, let's face it, I'm not stoked about driving a piece of junk truck or the fact that I learned to drive it yesterday.

"I can't, sweetie. I'm running behind and these two-lane roads are no joke with traffic."

Turning to Gran, "Gran?"

"Cadence, I have got to get started on tendin' to the animals this morning. The key is in the ignition like always, and from the looks of it yesterday, you'll be fine. Now go on before you're late."

"Fine," I say as my heels click on the wooden floor and I make my way toward her truck.

I open the door and decide I need a towel to sit on to be sure I don't get my skirt dirty. I run back in and grab one of the kitchen towels. As I turn the ignition, I pause. *What do I do?* I refuse to go back inside and ask Gran. Glancing at my watch, I have fifteen minutes until classes start. Taking a deep breath, I try to remember what Barrick told me. I take a moment and feel the truck. I stall out once at the stoplight in town when my heel slips from the gas pedal, so I quickly slide off my shoes and it makes driving easier. I arrive at school with five minutes to spare. Turning the ignition off, I make sure the emergency break is in place, slide my heels back on, and step out of the truck with my head held high. I did it.

Looking around, I can see that the transportation of choice is either a truck or small car. I also notice several are high-end vehicles. As I walk with confidence toward the office, I see the girl from The Loft and her posse. I smile and walk in the office, daring her to say something.

My schedule is a piece of cake. It looks like they have four classes each semester and my only academic class is English this semester. The secretary asks if I would like someone to show me around. I tell her no, and she gives me verbal directions. As I am walking out the door, a girl enters and smiles.

"Hey," she greets me.

I smile and reply back. I guess my assumption that people are polite in the South is correct as well. Let's see how many I get before I get to class. No joke. I swear someone spoke to me every two feet until I got to class.

The day goes as any first day would at any school. The teachers introduce themselves, go over rules and procedures, review the syllabi, and make us do some cheesy, get-to-know-you activity. By the time fourth block has started, I've tuned out most of it. As the bell is about to ring, the girl from this morning flies into class like a whirlwind.

"Sorry, Ms. Luckadoo," she says with a smile.

"That was close, Jade," she says as the girl takes a seat diagonal from me. She turns and says 'hey' to me yet again. What is it with these people?

As the bell rings for the end of the day, I stand and take my time walking from class because I don't want anyone to know I drive that clunker. I'm almost to the doorway when I hear Jade behind me.

"Hey, Cadence right?" she says.

I look at her. "Yup. That's me," I say with a fake smile. Why can't these people leave me alone?

"Just wanted to introduce myself. I'm Jade," she says as she walks beside me.

"Yeah. I got that from what's her face," I say, tossing my head back toward the classroom.

She giggles. "You're funny."

I crinkle my nose. I've never been called funny before. "Why's that?" I question.

"'Cause you just called Ms. Luckadoo, what's-her-face, and you look like you're about to run the catwalk at fashion week. You do realize where you are?"

"Well, I couldn't remember her name and I live for fashion. It's obvious people around here do not feel the same way."

"Oh they do, but it's different."

"What do you mean?"

Jade takes a moment to gather her thoughts. "Okay let me give you the run down." I can't wait to hear this. "Most girls around here are up on the latest southern, preppy trends from either Simply Southern, Southern Charm, or Southern Fried Chics. Every girl here owns boots to work in as well as boots to go out in. Jack Rogers are a must and we monogram everything."

"Are you serious? You monogram everything?"

"Yeah. Just look around." I do and notice every backpack as well as vehicle has initials on it. "Oh and don't forget the more glitter the better."

"That's insane. Are people afraid they are going to forget their names or something?" I say smartly.

"Nope, it's just a southern thang," she says with a deep southern drawl. "See," she says as she shows me her car. Oh gosh, she's one too.

"So tell me more about Lawndale High."

"Well, there's not much to say, I mean, it's school. The guys there are your typical country boys. They drive trucks and miss the first day of the season."

"Why would they miss school on the first day of autumn?" I question.

"Please tell me you didn't just say that."

"Um, yeah. The first season to occur while in school is autumn."

She starts to shake her head. "Girl, you've got a lot to learn around here. Let me spell it out for you. Bambi, big buck, big boy toys, trophies on the wall, and food in your belly."

I sit there and process it. "Ewwwww! Deer hunting?" I question in disgust. "Why would anyone want to hurt such a beautiful creature?"

"Bless it. You've got a lot to learn 'round here. Do you eat steak, chicken, veal?"

"Yeah."

"Same difference. I tell ya what, you've got to learn."

"What do you mean? Learn what?"

"I know you are fine being you, but some of those girls are brutal. They aren't nice at all. Not to mention life is different here. Expect to see a wide range of people, but most of them are plain 'ole country folks. They don't worry about impressing anyone. They do things differently down here. You need to be prepared for that because I'd hate for Maddie to start running her trap about you."

"Oh, you mean the girl that was talking smack at The Loft. I'm not worried about her," I say confidently, and I'm not. Only people who are insecure belittle others to stay on top.

"Yeah, about that—" I cut her off.

"Look, I know you were there. And I also know you didn't say anything about me. You aren't her and we're good," I say with a smile.

"Shew! I've been worrying about that since this morning."

"No worries. I can tell you're not like her, but why do you want to be friends with her?"

"Around here you keep your friends close, but your enemies closer."

Jade and I stand and talk for a few minutes. She glances at her watch and tells me she's got to go to practice. I bet she's a cheerleader. She tells me that tomorrow during lunch I should hang out with her, and I think that sounds like an awesome idea.

Glancing over my shoulder to make sure no one is watching, I hurry to the truck and escape without anyone noticing. Thank God!

BARRICK

As I'm cleaning out the storage closet in the barn and loading my truck with trash for the dump, I realize how thankful I am that I have all online classes and don't have to go in to school anymore. Just as my mind wanders to Cadence and her first day, I hear the truck pull up. Guess I taught her well, or at least well enough to get home. I give her a slight wave but get nothing in response as she struts to the house.

When I get back from the dump, I'm shocked to find Cadence in the barn talking on her phone.

"Oh my gosh Lauren, thank God you're home. Gran was about to drive me nuts with questions about the first day of school. It was awful! Those girls have no sense of fashion and they put their initials and glitter on everything. The only good thing was a girl named Jade that filled me in on everything, including the glitter." She laughs.

I clear my throat and she turns around. Seeing me there she walks past me and goes outside without a word. I hoped she would fill me in on her first day. Oh well. I finish working and go home.

CADENCE

I hop in Gran's truck, careful not to mess up my electric blue romper. Today I decided to wear flats so it would be easier to work the clutch. Arriving at school early, I take a deep breath hoping no one saw me in Gran's piece of junk. I grab the books I need for the day and close my locker.

"Well, looks like the fashionista doesn't have a fancy car to drive," Maddie says, looking me in the eye.

"Excuse me. Not only do you lack any kind of fashion sense, but I bet you drive a two-door sedan," I counter.

"Uh! You did not just call Bubbles a two-door sedan!" she says defensively. I burst out laughing and soon realize we have an audience.

"You freaking named your car? Who does that?" I laugh harder.

"And for the record it's not a sedan, it's a Mini Cooper." At this point, I try to refrain from speaking but it's no use.

"Let me get this straight. You drive a speck of a car that you've named Bubbles, your clothing is soooo three seasons ago on *Pretty Little Liars*, and you want to talk about my Gran's truck? It might be a piece of junk, but at least I look good driving it."

When she's speechless, I turn and make my way to class. Jade catches up with me.

"Holy crap, Cadence! I've never seen anyone talk to her that way."

"It's the truth. Plus, she might think she's all high and mighty, but there's nothing special about her."

"That's not how people 'round here see her. Maddie is like the queen bee and always gets what she wants."

"What do you mean?" I question.

"She's won homecoming court for our class like each year. She always has people falling at her feet, and she's got more money than most of us around here, well at least her family does. She won the

Miss Liver Mush Festival four years in a row and is hoping to win Miss Teen North Carolina if all goes according to her plan."

"What do you mean she's won for your class each year? Isn't that against the rules?" I ask.

"No, Maddie makes the rules."

"Hmm...I might have to see what I can do about that."

In the weeks leading up to homecoming, Maddie has been campaigning hard and has kept her distance from me. I've been passing the time playing pranks on Barrick in retaliation for the pranks he pulls on me. It's become our thing and how we deal with having to see each other every day. At school I get to see what Jade was talking about when she first told me about homecoming. There are signs everywhere. Girls have been talking about what they are going to wear, who they are going to the dance with, and I suddenly realize homecoming in the South is like the Super Bowl for teenage girls.

Jade and I have gotten closer and I pull her aside after class to get more information from her.

"These girls are serious about it, aren't they?" She laughs.

"Yes, they are. Are you going to go?"

"Yes, and now I need deets. Are you going shopping with me this weekend so I can find the right dress?" I question her.

There is hesitation in her voice. "Nah, I've got practice. Plus, my mom ordered one online for me."

"Practice? What sport practices on Saturday at school?" I ask.

"I dance."

Ah, she's a dancer. I wonder if that's why I like her so much. Maybe there's a secret dancer vibe I was picking up on.

"Oh really? Where do you train?"

"At the studio down the road. I've been going there since I could walk."

"Huh, cool." I wonder if she is any good training at that rinky-dink studio. Seriously, why couldn't Gran live closer to a big city so I could continue at a good school?

Jade and I go our separate ways and meet up for lunch. She tells me more about homecoming, and I can't believe it. Apparently, the entire town shuts down like they do every Friday night for football. Girls in the homecoming court leave school early to get their hair, makeup, and nails done. There's a parade downtown immediately after school, at halftime it's like a mini pageant, and once it's over everyone else leaves to get ready for the dance.

"So how does someone get on the court?" I ask her.

"People nominate and vote online," she says.

"Do you want to do it?"

She wiggles in her seat a little before she replies. "I mean... I'd like to, but what's the point? Maddie will win. She's won the past three years."

"She will not win this year. It's either going to be me or you, girlfriend," I state, pointing toward her.

"Well, I'll let you have that, Cadence," she says seriously.

"No, I don't know anything about this, and face it, I'm the new girl. You have the better shot at taking that high and mighty girl down."

"I don't know. She might be a mean girl, but I'm glad I'm in her acquaintance zone." Who would have thought that Jade would refer to herself as an acquaintance to Maddie? I can't believe she thinks that low of herself. I drop the subject, but know when I get home today I'm going to do my research, and this girl is going to leave a mark at homecoming. That's for sure.

When I get home, I use my phone to do as much digging as possible on Maddie. I search all of her social media platforms. I swear it's like she has people hypnotized around here. I shake my head.

"Whatcha doin'?" Gran asks as she enters the living room.

"Research."

"Care to share? I'm a pretty wise cookie," she says as she takes a seat beside me.

"I'm just finding out why everyone thinks Maddie is so special. Oh, and I'm trying to wrap my brain around homecoming. Gran, these girls are cray-cray! You'd think it was Miss America or something."

Gran laughs. "Maddie is from new money. I've seen her at The Loft. She seems to have a string of people following her, which isn't a good trait in my opinion. People should be who they are without someone telling them what's popular or not. I honestly think she's insecure. I've heard her mom isn't *stable.* As for homecoming, you really should ask your mother about that."

"You should ask me what?" Mom asks as she closes the front door.

"Cadence is asking about homecoming," Gran says with raised eyebrows.

Mom sets her purse on the coffee table and walks toward the fireplace mantel. "Cadence, you really want to go? I remember homecoming like it was yesterday. Homecoming court, the parade, the halftime show. The moment I saw Mandy Monroe win my freshman year, I knew I wanted to be queen. And, Cadence, dear, I achieved my goal," she says while pulling a picture out of a photo album.

I stare at it. The girl in the picture looks like me, but that dress is not something I'd be caught dead in. "Gran made my dress. We didn't have money to go and buy one. I know it's not your style, but when I was in school this dress set the trend for the years to come. Until that point, girls wore their Sunday best. I wouldn't settle for that and Gran can take a flat sheet and make it look like it belongs on the front page of Vogue."

I look at Gran. "Guilty," she says as she wiggles her fingers. "Your Gran's got deadly weapons right here."

"Mom, are you serious?" I ask, still unable to process it.

"As a heart attack." I sit and ponder that for a minute. I sure don't want to be homecoming queen, but I also know that I want to show Maddie who's the boss. I really think Jade needs to make it on the court. She's super nice and from what I can tell everyone likes her.

"I guess I need a dress," I say to Mom.

Gran jumps up. "Hold that thought." She hurries out of the room and comes back in with a box. She removes the lid and takes out a dress that is definitely older than me. "Whatcha think?" she questions.

"Ummmm." I don't know what to say. I'm sure that this is *the* dress in the picture, but it's not my style. "Gran, that's so twenty years ago," I say with attitude.

"Regina, you want to try it on?" Gran questions.

"I doubt I can fit in it."

"Come on," she says, handing it to Mom.

"Okay," Mom says and excuses herself.

When Mom returns, I'm in awe. Not only does it fit, but it is beautiful on her. I never knew my Gran could sew like that, but it's obvious where Mom's love for fashion came from.

"You look amazing, Mom."

"Lord have mercy! It's 'bout time you said something nice," Gran says to me.

I laugh. "It's the truth. My mom is beautiful, and Gran that dress is beautiful for her but *not* me. Mom, do you think there is any way you can call in a favor? I need a new dress that's hot off the runway."

"Welp, there it goes. I thought we were makin' progress, Cadence. Why can't you shop at the mall?"

I look at Mom with worry in my eyes. "A mall around here? I'd rather die. Besides, Jade didn't even shop around here. Her mom ordered one for her."

"I'll see what I can do," Mom says as she looks at herself in the mirror. For the first time since my dad walked out, I can see the light in my mom's eyes shine.

19

CADENCE

*A*t lunch the next day, Jade and I talk about running for homecoming queen. She seems unsure, but I think deep down she wants to run.

"Jade, seriously. It's obvious everyone loves you around here. Why not?" I question.

"Let's see. Maddie will make my life miserable."

"Screw her, you only have like eight months left until graduation. I'm nominating you," I say, then drop her name in the ballot box before she has time to react.

As I turn, Maddie is looking at me like she's plotting to kill me. I bet she thinks I'm nominating myself. How tacky would that be? I smile at her. She better start prepping for a fight because if Jade makes it to the final round of voting, she's going to win. I'm going to make sure of that.

The following day, they announce the votes and Jade is in the top three, just as I expected. For the rest of the week, Jade focuses on going out of her way to be nice to students and campaigning. We also go shopping so I can help her find the perfect shoes for her dress while I pray that Mom can come through with a dress for me. I've asked her every day, but she says to be patient. I suck at being patient.

At the end of the day on Thursday we vote for homecoming queen. If I could have stacked the votes I would have, but as Jade and I left fourth block, everyone we passed stopped to say they voted for her. *Please let her win. I'd just love to see the shock on Maddie's face.*

As we walk out to the parking lot, we talk about our plans for tomorrow. Gran and Mom are making me stay until the end of the day while Jade is leaving early to get "floosied up", as she says, before the parade. I shake my head; what is it with these strange words?

When I get home from school I'm surprised to see that Barrick's truck is gone. He's usually still here when I get home. Maybe he had to do something for school. I walk in the house and find Gran in the kitchen.

"Hey Gran. What are you making?"

"A pound cake."

"Yeah, I bet that will put on a pound or two."

She places her hand on her hip. Here we go. "I'll have you know that this recipe is healthy."

"Riiiight. What's healthy… the workout your arms are getting mixing the batter?" I say with a laugh.

She waves her hand in the air like I have no clue what I'm talking about, and I go to my room to do my homework when I get a text from Mom.

Mom: I'll be home soon. I've got a surprise for you.

Oh, thank God! Homecoming is tomorrow. I'd have a serious fashion emergency if she didn't. Unable to concentrate, I slip into my dance clothes, grab my iPod, and go outside to do what I enjoy most… dance.

As the sun begins to set, I see Mom coming down the driveway. I grab my iPod and sprint to her vehicle and pull her door open.

"Let me see!" I exclaim.

"Hold on one minute. Let me get in the house first," she says, opening the truck and removing a rectangular box.

"Ohmygosh, Mom, does that say Proenza Schouler?" She smiles. I knew Mom would come through, but this is amazing and I haven't even opened the box.

Walking in the house my patience thins, "Mom come on," I beg.

"Patience."

"I have none of that and you know it," I say as Gran comes to see what is going on.

"What in tarnation is going on in here?" she questions as I remove the top of the box. "Oh sweet Jesus!" she exclaims.

I take the shoulders of the dress and lift it from the box. The dress is a tightly woven cobalt gown that looks as if a string has been pulled at the bottom and it's unraveled past mid-thigh. It's elegant yet edgy. I notice the perfect heels to accent it are in the box as well.

"Mom it's beautiful, but how?"

"I called in a favor," she says with a wink.

"I'd hate to see why someone owed you a two-thousand-dollar-dress-with-matching-shoes favor." I laugh.

"Two thousand dollars! Regina, please tell me that's a joke," Gran says, looking a little pale.

"No Mom, Cadence is right, but I didn't pay for it. I called a friend that worked Fashion Week and she pulled a few strings. Don't you love it?" she asks Gran.

"I think I better sit down," she says, fanning herself. "For two thousand dollars it better love me back!"

Mom looks at me. "Go try it on."

I quickly run to my room and slide it on. It fits like a glove and as I look in the mirror, I feel like myself. I'm Cadence Lewis, dancer, girl with attitude, and ready to make Maddie's mouth hit the floor with envy. Walking back into the living room, Gran does a double take and looks at Mom.

"Mom, what do you think?" I ask as I twirl around in a circle. She stands and looks closely.

"It's breathtaking, Cade. I love it!" she says and looks at Gran.

"You got panties on under that thing?" she questions.

"What?" I ask confused. Why is that any of her business?

She begins to spell it out for me. "Do you have underwear, draw-ers, bloomers, under garments, or even a thong?" I cover my ears; Gran just said *thong*! Mom looks at her like she's crazy. "Honey, you're gonna show all your goods if you're not careful. I'm just trying to make sure you're covered up. I mean, I know things are different these days, but at least leave something to the imagination."

"MOTHER!" My mom gasps.

"Hey, I'm just calling it like I see it, and if she bends over without anything on, everyone is going to see the Promised Land with those slits."

"Yes, I've got panties on, thank you!" I say to Gran. This dress completely covers me up top but it has slits almost to the top of my legs, so a pair of dance shorts will put Gran at ease.

I turn to go to my room to change when there is a knock on the door. "Come in," Gran yells without seeing who it is. What if it's an axe murder or something? I laugh at that thought. I bet not one crime has been committed in this town ever.

BARRICK

I enter Ms. Mae's and almost trip over my chin when I see Cadence in a dress that clings to her body and barely covers her behind. I blink and quickly close my mouth as I try not to stare. She's always dressed to the hilt, but tonight she looks amazing. I have to look away when I hear Ms. Mae clear her throat.

"Hey, Ms. Mae. I wanted to let you know that I just got back and put Daisy back in the pasture. The vet said she's pregnant and about three months along."

"Thank you, Barrick. Did the vet say everything looked okay?" Ms. Mae questions as she stands and I notice that Cadence has slipped away.

"He said everything looked great but we need to keep checking her. She's due near the end of April."

"Great. Are you okay with doing that or should I?"

"Either way," I reply as Cadence enters the room in regular clothes.

"What are you checking?" she questions.

"Daisy, the cow, is pregnant. We have to make sure she and the calf are okay," Gran says.

"How do you know she's pregnant?" Cadence asks. I laugh. I know she can figure that out but I can't resist messing with her.

"Basically we locked her and bull number fifty-four in a pen and let them go at it," I say with a straight face. Her face molds into a look of horror and Ms. Mae looks at me while covering her mouth trying not to laugh.

"He's not serious is he, Gran?"

"Heck no! It was more like Barrick caught them in the pasture back in July."

"Ohmygosh! I can't hear this!" she says, hurrying out of the room. I can't help but stare as her backside moves up the staircase and vanishes. As I turn to Ms. Mae she has her finger pointing at me.

"You should be ashamed, young man. I'll give you credit it was funny, but bless poor Cadence's heart she's never experienced any of this. I'm sure it's a lot to take in, and you knew exactly what you were doing. Oh, and quit checking out her backside."

"Sorry Ms. Mae. It's just—"

"I know about all of your pranks. That's why I let you go ahead with it, but if I were you, I'd watch out. I would even sleep with an eye open." She laughs.

"Oh and tomorrow, I need to leave in time for the parade. I'll make sure that everything's finished before then. Is that okay?" I ask, already knowing the answer.

"Oh course! I wouldn't dare dream of makin' you work while everyone else in this town plays. Not to mention, I might need to hitch a ride myself."

CADENCE

Swiftly escaping Barrick and his disgusting jokes, I call Lauren. I leave out the details of Daisy because no one needs to be exposed to that. I give her complete details of my dress, all of the homecoming festivities, and how I pray that Jade will beat Maddie.

"Who's Jade?" she questions with a hint of jealousy in her voice.

"Oh, she's like the only person I've actually had a conversation with off the farm."

"Oh," she says shortly.

"What's your deal?" I banter back.

"Nothing. I hope that you're not going to drop your standards on friends since you're there."

"Of course not, but get this. She dances at that hillbilly studio Gran wants me to visit."

"Shut up!" she exclaims.

"No joke. I can't wait to see her dance tomorrow." I laugh and Lauren follows suit. "There is no way that she's as good as me."

"Uh, not even a little bit," Lauren says before she fills me in on everything at home. I notice the time and realize I have to get ready for bed. Tomorrow is game day and I'm not talking about football. I tell Lauren I have to go but will call her after the dance.

20

CADENCE

*J*ade leaves after lunch along with half of the students. I can't believe that Gran and Mom made me stay until the end of the day, but I quickly get over it. When the three o'clock bell rings, I walk to the truck and drive to Lawndale.

From what Jade has told me the parade isn't that long, but everyone will be there. She wasn't kidding. By three thirty the streets are lined with people. Who knew there were this many people in town? I see Barrick on the other side of the street standing with Gran. *Did she ride with him?* Obviously, I have her truck. Gran waves at me and I look both ways before I go to meet her.

"Are you excited?" she asks me.

"It's just a parade," I say, waiting for it to start.

"Honey, just wait. This is just the beginning of it," she says giddily while quickly clapping her hands.

Cars start to flow down the street as the parade begins. The line starts with clubs and organizations followed by the class representatives. I've never seen so much big hair in my life! Didn't they know that died in the eighties?

As the senior homecoming court approaches, I look for Jade. She is in an old Mustang convertible. Her hair is perfect, not too big like the others, and she's smiling from ear to ear.

"Look, Gran! It's Jade. The girl I was telling you about. Doesn't she look gorgeous?" I ask.

"She does. What do you think, Barrick?" Gran asks.

"She looks pretty, I guess," he says before turning to talk to a group of guys that I assume are his friends.

Jade finds me in the crowd and smiles even bigger. I'm so glad I didn't give her a choice: she's totally got this. When I see Maddie, her hair is in a poof the size of our barn and there are so many sequins on her dress that I'm blinded from the reflection. Someone should really tell her less is more. She waves at me and I'm in shock until I see Barrick and his friends give her a slight nod.

When the parade is over, I go home and relax a little before the game starts. I have it timed perfectly so that I can shower and get ninety percent ready before the game.

Gran, Mom and I ride to the game together. I wear a pair of skinny jeans and a top. Gran is head to toe in school apparel that is at least thirty years old. I shake my head as I get in Mom's Suburban.

When we get to school, the parking lot is full and the stands are packed. I take a seat beside Mom and we watch as the game begins. At halftime, the homecoming nominees line the field and I hold my breath as the queen is revealed.

The announcer comes through the speaker. "Your 2015 homecoming queen is Jade…" and that's all I hear as the stands go crazy. I look to Maddie, who is in complete shock. "Goodie," I say as I look at Gran and Mom. "Told you guys she'd win."

"That you did," Gran says with a smile.

Jade makes her way to me and I hug her. I'm glad I have her since I can't be with Lauren. When there are a few minutes left in the fourth quarter we get ready to leave to beat the traffic. Jade asks if I want her to come help me get ready, but I know that if she leaves now she'll regret it later. Now is her time to shine.

As soon as we get home, I go upstairs to touch up my makeup and hair. I carefully slide on my dress, add the perfect accessories and slip my feet in the heels. I take a deep breath and look in the mirror before heading downstairs. I look fabulous!

Gran and Mom are waiting at the bottom of the steps.

"Hold on right there. Let me get your picture," Mom says. "I promised I'd send it to your..." she stops mid-sentence.

"Who?"

"Your dad. He needs to see this." Just like that my mood flips and I don't care about him seeing me in this dress.

"Mom, he hasn't even called me yet. Why does he deserve to have a glimpse into our lives?"

"Because he's your father. Now smile," she says as she holds up her phone. Just as she's about to snap it, I make a face in the camera.

"Cadence!" Mom shouts.

"What? I thought that was fitting? What do you think, Gran?" I question because I know she hates him as much as I do. Wouldn't any mother hate their cheating ex son-in-law?

"Hold on a minute," Gran says as she comes to stand beside me. "Now Regina, take one of the both of us." Mom looks nervous as Gran smirks at me. As Mom tells us to get ready, Gran whispers for me to do that again. When the flash happens Gran and I both make faces in the camera and Mom comes unglued.

"I can't believe you two!" she exclaims.

"Well, I never liked him anyways," Gran says.

I start to laugh. "Mom you should come do a selfie with us. I promise it feels good." She shakes her head no, but then gives in. We laugh and it feels good. Afterward Mom asks me to take a serious picture. I do, and when I walk down the porch steps they both tell me I look beautiful. Mom gives me the keys to her car, and I drive to school.

The parking lot is full and the stadium lights are still on, but there isn't a soul over there. I hear music coming from the gym. *I can't believe I'm going to a school dance in a gym.* I scan the parking lot for Jade's car and I see her walking toward me.

"Cadence, you look amazing!" she says.

"Thanks, so do you! So how does it feel to be homecoming queen?" I ask her.

"Fan-freakin-tastic," she says as she loops her arm through mine and we laugh as we walk toward the gym door.

I'm in awe that the gym has been transformed to look like I just stepped into a fairytale. I look around to see if Prince Charming is waiting for me, but that thought quickly fades when I only see teenage boys in slacks and button down shirts. I do have to say they clean up pretty well.

Jade and I walk around and she is stopped every few steps by classmates congratulating her. As more students arrive, we find a seat at a table to sit and talk. I'm amazed how everyone is just sitting around and not on the dance floor. That's when I see Maddie and her posse. They walk in like they own the place, and up until now she has. I nudge Jade.

"Oh lawd, I sure hope she's not walking over here to run her mouth some more," Jade says.

"What do you mean?" I question.

"After you left the game she tried to have a not-so-friendly conversation with me, but it didn't go as she hoped. I swear, one day she's going to realize she has no one. Right now she has a few people that think she's the best thing 'round here, and I used to be like that. Not after tonight. I've seen that I can be me, and people like it. Thank you, Cadence. If you hadn't nominated me, I wouldn't be here."

I'm almost at a loss of words. I nominated her because I wanted her to beat Maddie, but I didn't realize what it really meant to her. I have a flash of guilt, but it quickly fades.

"It was nothing. I knew you wanted to, but just needed someone to push you in that direction. Oh, and if she runs her mouth, we've got this," I say as the music changes to a new country song.

"Oh my gosh! I love this song," Jade says and tries to get me to dance. I shake her off. I'm not dancing to that. Jade dances with a group of girls and as the music slows down I see Aaron ask her to dance.

Almost everyone is on the dance floor and I feel out of my element. I've never been on the sidelines at a school dance. I've always been one of the first ones with a date. As the music changes to an upbeat country song all of the girls squeal and I see a line dance breaking out. I shake my head as Maddie walks by.

"So, you too good for us? I'd think a girl like you liked to have a good time," she says in a condescending tone and something in me cracks. I watch as everyone lines up in a row and does the same steps over and over. I count the beat in my head, watch their feet for two eight counts, and take a deep breath. I can't believe I'm going to do this, but it's time that she knew exactly who she's messing with.

I stand and walk toward Jade on the dance floor. "Do you know this?" she asks. I shrug my shoulders. I join in like I've been doing this for years and don't miss a beat or turn. After we make it through the line dance one full time, I decide to step it up a notch, and throw in a little extra spice. When the song ends, Jade looks at me. "You've been holding out on me," she says with her hands on her hips.

"Nah, I just watched a few eight counts, and made it a little more Cadence-like," I say with a smile just before I feel a tap on my shoulder.

"So, that all you got?" Maddie quips.

"Are you serious right now? It's a freaking country line dance. It's not rocket science. I figured you'd be over your high-and-mighty self by now. I mean, please. You aren't as great as you think you are, and people around here know it," I say as her mouth falls open and she turns around without another word.

"That was awesome," Jade says.

"It's the truth, and it's time someone stood up to her. I've got a question, do they play other music besides country?" I ask.

"Oh yeah. You just have to ask. They start out with country, but they will play anything, even the Wobble. Whatcha thinkin'?"

"Did you say Wobble?" She nods her head yes. Um, that's so two years ago, and that's when I see Maddie walk to the DJ, and as the song ends the Wobble begins to play. Jade and I look at each other and begin to laugh. "Come on," I say to her as we hit the dance floor, but not before I stop and request a song.

Jade and I both follow in line and it's obvious that she's a dancer, and that Maddie has major white-girl dancing issues. I can't wait to see what happens when my request comes on. As the song ends, a hard beat begins to play and everyone looks at each other. I look at Jade and she reads my mind. We begin to dance and don't care who is watching, but it's obvious that everyone's eyes are on us, especially Maddie's. I laugh when I see her cross her arms and walk toward a table. She couldn't hang with us if her life depended on it.

As the song ends, the rap is replaced with country again, and we exit the dance floor and take a seat.

"That was awesome, Cadence! You seriously have been holding out on me. You're amazing and you should come to the studio with me. I'm sure it's not what you're used to, but you should at least try it," Jade says.

"I don't know. I'm not sure I can."

"What do you mean?" she questions.

"I promised I wouldn't. It's my senior year and everything is so different. It doesn't feel right, and not to mention I don't know what dancing at a small studio is going to do for my career."

Jade's eyes about bug out of her head. "Career? Well, I can promise you this. Not dancing at all will not help your career. We might be small, but Ms. Lyndsay is amazing. We compete on a competitive level everywhere we go, and have a trophy case full of Crystals." *Seriously?*

"Are you serious?"

"Now why would I lie about that? Please, just go with me and see," she pleads.

"I don't know."

"Well, think about it," she says.

21

CADENCE

I'm exhausted from homecoming, and Gran has the nerve to wake me up before the crack of dawn to help her on the farm. I reluctantly slide out of bed, put on her old boots and follow her to the barn. Wiping my eyes, I notice that Barrick isn't here, and I find that strange. He's been here every day since I've arrived.

"Cadence, I need you to bring in the cows for milkin'," she says.

"You what?" I ask, knowing I didn't hear her correctly.

"Girl, you heard me. Go get the cows."

"Isn't this Barrick's job?" I question.

"Barrick has the day off. He's gone fishing up the mountains with some friends. You, my dear, are going to help me 'round here today and tomorrow."

"Gran! Do you know what happened the last time I had to help Barrick?"

She smirks. "Doesn't matter. I'm going to show you how it's done. Now come on, daylight's burnin' and I don't plan on being in this barn all day."

I slowly follow Gran into the milking stations. I watch as she gets everything ready. She turns to look at me. "Cadence, go get the cows, honey." Well, this morning isn't starting off as I planned.

I bring the cows in, only touching them when absolutely necessary. Gran has the station ready to go and insists that I help her. She gives me direct instructions on what to do, and I am amazed at how different this is than working with Barrick. She is straightforward, doesn't try to prank me, and she's down to business. Before I know it, I've successfully milked a cow and we are done for the morning.

When she begins to clean up, I offer to help without being told. Gran smiles at me. When we finish, we head to the house. I smell coffee and pancakes as we walk into the kitchen.

Gran offers to help Mom but she insists we take a seat. She finishes the pancakes and sets them in front of us. My mom's pancakes are my favorite because she makes them low fat and high in protein just for me.

I get to relax for the remainder of the day so I watch TV, dance in my room, and call Jade to see what she is doing. She doesn't answer and I can only assume she's at dance. A few hours later she calls me and confirms my assumption. She tells me that she's going to The Loft tonight and I should, too. I, however, do not have that on my agenda. I believe I'll stay home and catch up on the latest Lifetime movie because Gran has already informed me that I'll be back at the barn before the rooster crows in the morning.

BARRICK

It's strange being away from Ms. Mae's farm all weekend. I almost feel lost. It's my first day off in six months. Aaron and a few guys invited me to go camping and fishing this weekend in the mountains. I couldn't resist after having to attend all of the homecoming festivities yesterday. I swear, I never liked watching all of that when I was in school, but I also know it's what our town is about.

We arrived at our campsite around ten last night since we had to wait around to find out who was crowned homecoming queen. Luckily for us we aren't really roughing it. Aaron's parents have a permanent site, so everything was ready when we arrived. It would not have been fun at all to have to set up a tent that late at night.

We are sitting around the campfire preparing our fishing gear when I think about the look on Maddie's face when she didn't win last night. I always knew Jade had it in her to stand up for herself. My mind quickly wanders to Cadence and her dress. She looked amazing and I wish I could have had a dance with her. I don't think Cadence realizes it yet, but she's making an impression on this town. I wish she'd come around and realize that Delight isn't so bad.

"Dude, are you comin' or what?" Aaron asks.

"Yeah," I say as I grab my fishing rod and head to the lake.

We sit back and relax as we wait for the fish to bite. I'm so happy I'm not milking a cow right now.

"So what can you tell us about that new girl?" Sam asks.

"What do you mean?" I question.

"You've been around her. She's hot." Sam states the obvious and I start to laugh.

"She's hot all right. She's got a hot temper and I'd hate to cross her. She's a lot like Ms. Mae but she needs a lesson in the respect department."

"I'd hate to be her 'cause Ms. Mae doesn't handle that well I'm sure," Aaron laughs.

"You're right. She's made her work every day on the farm since she arrived. Y'all should have seen her when I had her clean the stalls."

"Please tell me you didn't make it hard on her?" Aaron asks.

"Yeah I did. The way she ran her mouth she deserved it, and when she landed her rear in a pile of cow manure, I'd have paid money to have that on video."

"Barrick, you're kiddin' right?" Sam asks.

"Nope, and we've been making each other's lives miserable ever since."

They all look at each other and I know exactly what they are thinking. They think I like Cadence. Maybe I do, but messing with her is just too much fun to stop and I'd believe she'd say the same thing.

22

CADENCE

*S*unday afternoon Gran sends me to do the milking. She says
that I can handle one session by myself, and if so, she might
ease up on me. I'm taking that for what it's worth and working today
no matter how much I hate it.

As I usher in the last set of cows, I'm surprised to see Barrick
walking into the barn. Seriously, he needs to learn what a weekend off
means. I can promise you that if Gran told me to take time off, I
wouldn't come back until the last minute.

"Well, well. Now isn't this a sight," he says with a smirk and I
ignore him. "So that's how it's gonna be?" he questions and I continue
to ignore him. "I go away for a day and you turn into the golden
child?"

"No. Gran said if I did this myself she'd lighten my load," I say
smartly.

"I see. You're a what's-in-it-for-me kinda girl," he says and I don't
answer.

As I finish, I stand and take them back out to the pasture. When I return, Barrick has begun to clean up the equipment.

"You don't have to do that. If Gran sees you then her deal is off. I can't afford to let that happen," I say as I start to clean up and Barrick reluctantly stops.

"So how was the dance?" he questions as my phone begins to ring. *Who in the world could that be?* Taking it from my pocket, I'm shocked when I see Dad on the screen.

"I'll be right back." I answer the call and walk out of the barn. "Hey Dad."

"Hey Cadence. How are you?" *Oh, you finally decided to call.*

"I'm fine. What do you want?"

"I wanted to see how you were. I'm sorry I haven't called. I've just been busy."

"Oh I bet. Busy with what's-her-face."

"Cadence, do you have to be like this?" he says, aggravated.

"Be like what? Dad, I've been gone for like two months and you haven't called me once. I'm smart enough to know that she's left you or you feel bad about something."

He gets quiet for a moment. "Cadence, your mom sent me your picture from homecoming and I wanted to know how it went. I'd also like you to come for a visit. What do you think?"

"It went fine. Sure, I'll come but is *she* going to be there when I come?" I ask.

"Cadence, you're going to have to accept that Mindy is going to be around for a long time," he says.

"If you say so. Look, I've got to go. Call me when know you the details," I say as I disconnect and scream in frustration.

BARRICK

I hear Cadence holler like she is being torn into a million pieces and drop what I am doing and run outside.

"Cadence, are you okay?"

She looks at me and hurt flashes in her eyes as anger begins to replace it. "I'm fine."

"Um, I'm no genius and I don't claim to understand girls at all but that sound was not fine."

"Of course, a guy would try and fix the problem. Funny thing is men can't fix this problem. They *are* the problem."

I have no idea what she means by that. I mean I haven't been nice to her, but I didn't make her yell like that. "Look, I'm not sure what's going on. I heard you from inside the barn and I thought something had happened to you. Obviously, I was wrong. Sorry for attempting to be a good guy," I say as I turn to leave.

Cadence doesn't return to the barn and when I finish cleaning, I see that she's on the front porch with her mother. I can only assume that she knows what's going on, and I hope and pray that she knows how to help her.

CADENCE

I feel emotionally exhausted Monday morning when I wake up. Crying that many tears in one night can do that to a person. I absolutely hate my dad. I was beginning to move on from the fact that he hadn't called to check on me and then he just swoops in and asks me to come for a visit. If he's too busy to call me on a regular basis then he should stay busy and out of my life. Why can't he just leave me alone?

I look terrible so I take extra time to apply my concealer. By the time I get downstairs I realize Gran isn't in the house and Mom has already left. I pour a cup of coffee and roll my eyes as I walk toward Gran's truck. Rolling your eyes really hurts when they are already puffy. Maybe I should stop doing that so much.

Jade is waiting for me in the parking lot when I get to school. As soon as I'm within speaking distance she's nagging me about dance.

"So, Cadence you're coming with me to the studio today, aren't you?" she asks.

"Jade, I didn't bring my clothes."

"I've got plenty."

"I'd rather have my own," I banter back.

"Fine, then why don't I pick you up and we ride together?" There is no way she's letting me out of this.

"I'll have to call Gran. She has me working every afternoon. She might not let me," I say, knowing I'll have to call during lunch.

The entire time I'm in class all I can think about is what it will be like to dance somewhere else. I wonder if Gran will let me go and if I do go, if I'll make any new progress.

I call Gran from the bathroom at lunchtime since cellphones aren't allowed in school. I'm surprised when a male voice answers the phone.

"Barrick?" I question.

"Speaking," he says.

"Where is Gran?" I ask because I've never known him to answer the phone.

"She's in the powder room. We're about to eat lunch," he says.

"Oh. I need to talk to her," I say as I hear her in the background.

"Cade, everything okay?" she questions, taking the phone.

"I'm fine, but I have a question. My friend Jade wants me to go to that rinky-dink studio and won't take no for an answer. I told her I needed to check with you." Deep down I'm praying she says I have to stay at the farm.

"Sure! Do you want me to have Barrick bring your clothes by the school?" she asks. Something about him holding my personal belongings makes me uneasy.

"I'll come home after school. I think I'm going to ride with her as well," I say.

"Okay. Just let me know when to expect you home tonight, and you are still responsible for helping out on the farm, too."

"Okay. I'll see you this afternoon," I say as I hang up.

Walking into the cafeteria I look for Jade and take a seat beside her. She just stares at me.

"What?" I question.

"And?" she asks, wanting to know what Gran said.

"I can go. Just meet me at my Gran's. She lives at—"

"I know where Ms. Mae lives. Everyone 'round here does," she says with a laugh.

BARRICK

"Everything okay?" I ask Ms. Mae.

"Yeah, I think. Cadence finally decided to check out that studio down the road and asked if she could go. I hope they are ready for her," she says with a laugh. "I told her you could bring her stuff, but she vetoed that."

I take a bite of my sandwich. Cadence doesn't want me near her stuff. That's not a shocker.

"You know I think it will be good for her, Barrick. What do you think?" she asks me.

Why is she asking me this? "I don't know, but at least she's being more respectful these days."

"Awe! You know she's just pretending, don't ya?" Ms. Mae says and I choke on my tea. That hadn't really crossed my mind. "Bless it Barrick. She's just doing what I ask because she wants me to loosen the reigns a little."

I sit there quietly and take it all in. It's all an act. I make a mental note to remember that when I see her working so hard with a smile on her face. And here I thought she was actually letting her guard down and embracing Delight.

Ms. Mae stops me before I head back out to the barn. "Barrick, I need to go to the bank. Would you mind taking me?"

"Of course not. I'll take you as soon as I finish the afternoon milking."

24

CADENCE

*B*y the time the bell rings for the end of the day, I'm not as relieved as I hoped I'd be. Gran said I could go to dance but I still have to help on the farm. I know I need to get it together but I don't know if I can. How can I when I have dance, homework *and* farm work to do? I quickly call Lauren on my way home to vent. She wishes me good luck and to not take any crap off of any two-stepping country line dancers. We both laugh and then I hang up when I get in the driveway. I am surprised that Barrick and Gran aren't home.

Walking in the house, I see that Gran has left a note on the table in the foyer. *Gone to bank. Barrick drove.* I put it back on the table and hurry to my room. I toss my backpack on my bed and grab my dance bag that luckily has always been packed. I take a deep breath and hustle down to Jade's car.

As I open the door, I catch a glimpse of Barrick's truck coming up the drive, and I feel the irritation rise. As we pass Barrick, Jade gives him a smile and a wave. Please tell me she's not into him. He's such an pain.

"Ugh! Can't he just pick some beans or something?" I say in frustration as I turn from looking at Barrick.

Jade begins to laugh. "I take it Barrick hasn't turned on his charm?"

"Yeah, I don't think I'd call stalking someone charm."

She looks at me strangely. "What do you mean?" she asks with concern in her voice.

"Never mind. I mean if you want him, pleeeease take him."

Jade looks at me with a blank look and then bursts out laughing until she's crying.

"What's so funny, Jade?" I ask, feeling like the butt of a joke.

"Nothing. He's just not my type," she says, trying to gather herself.

Jade doesn't say anything else for a few minutes, but turns up the radio, and of course it's country.

"Can we listen to something else?" I ask.

"Sure. I just thought I'd drive you crazy," she says with a laugh as she hits a preset button for a local pop station. I've never been so happy to hear Selena Gomez in my life.

After a few songs, Jade turns down the volume. "When we get there, Ms. Lyndsay will be at the desk. I'll introduce you. She's amazing. Seriously, I've never seen anyone move like her."

"I bet I have," I say with attitude. Jade looks at me like she wants to say something but she keeps her thoughts to herself.

When we get in the studio, Jade introduces me to the instructor, who is in phenomenal shape. She's lean and it's obvious she still dances on a daily basis. "Hi Cadence. My name is Lyndsay, and I'm the owner of Stars Dance Academy. We offer a wide range of levels and classes. What type of classes are you lookin' into?" she says with a southern twang.

"I have been dancing since I was two, and have been taking intensive lessons in ballet, tap, jazz, contemporary, and hip hop. I've competed at the competitive level since I was four years old, and have been working with my duet partner, Lauren, since we were minis. I'm a senior this year, and planned on joining a company based off of my senior routine. Well, until I was forced to move here," I say with more attitude than I had planned.

"That's impressive, Cadence. We have students of all levels here." *Great, here we go.* "We also have had students work with Joffrey Ballet School as well as the University of North Carolina School of the Arts. We take pride in being a small town studio that can compete with the larger cities. Come on, let me show you around."

I follow her and Jade excuses herself to get ready for class. She shows me the break room and two studio rooms. One is large and the other is smaller. The floor is worn and the building is musty-smelling. She then shows me a class schedule and says that I'm more than welcome to observe or participate in class today.

Unsure of how I feel about this, I want to say no but I also am dying to dance on the wooden floor with mirrors the entire length. I want to critique my moves and find others that believe dance is the most important thing in the world. I want to dance.

"Okay," I say as I look at Lyndsay. She smiles and leads me to the break room. Jade shows me where I can store my belongings and then a few other girls enter the room. She introduces me to them and then we get ready for class to begin.

We start with our stretches just like any other class I've attended. When Lyndsay gives directions, I follow perfectly. It's obvious by the look on her face that she's impressed. When we take a break, she stops me.

"Cadence, your technique is amazing."

"Thanks. Like I said, I've been training since I was two and competitive since I was four so I take dance pretty seriously," I say before I turn and get a drink of water.

Jade stops me at the water fountain. "What's your deal?" she questions.

"What do you mean?"

"How about you drop that chip off your shoulder and enjoy the next few hours," she says, and I take a deep breath so that I don't say anything inappropriate.

"Look, I just don't know how a lady from here has that much experience but at this point I'll take what I can get. You said yourself I have to keep doing something." Jade starts to comment, but we are called back into the room.

Over the next two hours, we work on turns, leaps, and flexibility. Our last exercise was an impromptu session where a variety of music was played and we had to improvise.

"Cadence, that was excellent, but what if you took some of that emotion and twisted it like this?" Ms. Lyndsay suggests as she shows me a more graceful move. Being raw and edgy has always been my forte.

"Thanks but no thanks," I say, moving to the opposite end of the room. Jade shows a flash of concern on her face.

"Can I speak to you in my office, Cadence?" Ms. Lyndsay asks in an authoritative voice. *Great.*

She takes a moment to gather her words, but I can see the anger rising. I try to refrain from laughing.

"I know you think that you're better than this studio, but let me inform you of one thing. We are the best. These girls work hard each and every day to go above and beyond what I ask of them. You can either follow suit or not return tomorrow."

Looking around, I notice a picture with a familiar-looking building. "What's that?" I question and I can see her irritation flare yet again.

"Respect, Cadence. You might need to look up the definition before you return tomorrow," she says and we both walk back to class.

After another forty-five minutes, we are dismissed for the night. Jade and I are sweating messes, and it feels amazing.

When we get in her car, Jade turns to me. "What the world?" She says and I look at her like I'm clueless. "Drop the act. I brought you here because I thought it would be good for you, but you had to be a bitty to Ms. Lyndsay. You aren't better than her or us."

I feel the anger rise in my cheeks. I am better than them. "I think I did amazing in there tonight."

"Agreed, but you didn't have to have that high and mighty attitude. Ms. Lyndsay has given up a lot to be where she is right now. You might need to get off your high horse and think about other people for five minutes."

"What do you mean?" I question.

"Ms. Lyndsay got into Juilliard, but her mom was killed. Her dad wasn't in the picture and she had a brother that wasn't eighteen. She gave up her dream so he wouldn't have to go in foster care. She came home, took classes at the local community college and opened the studio. Life doesn't always go as planned, but sometimes you have to take what's left and move forward."

I suddenly realize where the photo in her office was taken. There were three girls standing outside a performing hall, Juilliard. Suddenly, I feel ashamed of myself.

"I didn't know," I whisper to Jade.

"I know, but next time before you act like you're better than others, do your research. I told you we were the best and she's why."

Our ride home is quiet, and I don't know what to say to her. I realize I've been wrong about several things. When she drops me off at the house, I look at her before getting out of the car. "So can I ride with you tomorrow?" I ask.

"Of course, just leave that snotty attitude in the barn," she says with a laugh.

I wave bye to Jade and enter the house to find Mom and Gran waiting to eat dinner with me.

"How was it?" Mom asks.

"Fine, but I think I might have misjudged that place."

"I told ya!" Gran says and I cut my eyes to her.

"Did you know that the instructor went to Juilliard?" I ask Gran.

"Yup. I don't know much about this dance stuff, but I know about Juilliard. You just never bothered to ask me. It's too bad about her mom. To have to put your life on hold to take care of your brother like she did. That's just sad," she says as she shakes her head.

Gran excuses herself and I can tell that Mom is waiting for more information from me that isn't related to dance.

"Heard any more?" she asks, referring to Dad.

"Nope," I say as I stand to leave and avoid the conversation.

"Have a seat." I still consider running to my room because I don't want to talk about him but I decide to be respectful and sit. "He sent me an email today. He mentioned he wants you to visit for Thanksgiving," she says.

"What do you want me to do?" I question Mom.

"Whatever you feel the most comfortable with. Gran and I would miss you but at least if you went, you could see Lauren." She has a point.

I take out my phone and text him that I'll come. Of course, I don't hear anything. I would at least expect some response since he's the one who asked me to come.

BARRICK

This past month I've kept an eye on Cadence and noticed she's different. She still doesn't love milking the cows, but she doesn't seem to have that chip on her shoulder like she used to. Ms. Mae talks about her nonstop during the day. She tells me how she's doing at the studio and how she's making new friends. She also mentioned that she is going to ease up on Cadence during the week so she can get her homework and dance practice in, and work more on the weekends. I hope Cadence is really trying this time. I think it would really hurt Ms. Mae's feelings if she were just putting up a front to get what she wants. I guess time will tell.

25

CADENCE

*J*ade and I have a new ritual now that we are in dance together. She picks me up every morning so we can go directly to the dance studio after school. Since my first day, I've decided to give the place a chance. In fact, it's the only place I remotely fit in. I can honestly say that dance makes the world go round. My phone calls with Lauren have become less frequent, and I can tell that she's moving on without me. She mentioned a few auditions coming up for her. I'm happy for her, but it sucks for me.

Gran has lightened my load to only three mornings a week and the weekends. I still think that's a lot and the thought of getting up before five in the morning is killing me. Knowing I can't even sleep in on Saturdays makes it even worse. I'd love to be able to sleep in.

On Saturday morning, I'm pulled from my sleep by my alarm clock. I reluctantly roll out of bed, put on clothes, and slide on Gran's boots. I swear wearing them is beginning to become second nature, I just wish there weren't so big and more my style.

Barrick is already here when I walk into the barn. Great.

"Mornin'," he says as he leads the cows into the milking stations.

"Hey." I say as I walk toward him and begin to attach the cups. He stops and looks at me. "You got a problem?" I say looking at him.

"Nope," he says as he continues to work and then mumbles under his breath something about a tutu.

"What did you say?"

"Nothin'," he says, turning to his work.

"If you have something to say, by all means, please lay it out there."

"It's nothing. I'm just surprised I didn't have to tell you what to do. I thought once Ms. Mae gave in to you going to the studio, you'd be slacking off 'round here."

"I might be able to go to the studio, but I have to spend my weekends working on the farm." He stops working and turns to look at me. His lips are pressed together like he's trying to gather his words, but refrains before he turns toward the cow to continue working.

"Look, I don't like being out here anymore than you like me being out here. Let's just do what we have to do and get done," I say with my arms crossed.

"So are you being helpful because you want to help or because you want to dance?" he asks.

"What does it matter to you as long as I pull my weight?"

"I guess it doesn't," he states and continues to milk the cows.

I leave him alone in the milking station and decide to start cleaning the stalls. I take my time, and before long he is working beside me.

"I don't need your help."

"The faster we both do this, the faster we're done." He does have a point.

We are almost finished when I hear my cellphone chime. I put the pitchfork down to see who it is. Barrick shakes his head at me.

"Seriously!" I say looking at the screen as I read a text from my dad.

Dad: Sorry. Something's come up for Thanksgiving. Maybe Christmas?

I turn to start back to work when I realize that Barrick is staring at me. "What?" I huff.

"Everything okay?"

"Not really."

"Sorry."

"Sorry? How can you be sorry for something that has nothing to do with you?"

"I was just trying to be nice."

"Whatever! All men are the same. You try to make up once you mess up but then you mess up all over again."

"What are you talkin' 'bout?" Barrick asks as he steps closer.

"Guys! You all say one thing and mean another or just do stupid stuff to piss me off."

"What? Like this?" Barrick says as he pulls me in for a kiss. I give in because his lips are so soft and he has me pulled in tightly. I suddenly realize what I'm doing and pull away.

"What in the world?" I try to walk away from him but he pulls me in for a hug.

BARRICK

I don't know what made me do it, but when she started talking like that, I just had to shut her up. I wanted to make her feel better and show her that not all guys are the same. I know she liked it; I felt her give in to the kiss. I wish she'd let me in.

"Sorry. You just wouldn't be quiet," I say as I step away from her.

"Do you normally do that to people when they are having a meltdown?"

I smirk because that was a first. "Nah, I don't think most of the guys would appreciate that," I say as I turn back to the stall. I can feel her eyes on me, so I turn back to face her.

"So just like that, you're going back to work like you didn't just attack my lips?" she asks. I continue to work without a word. "For the record, if you ever touch my lips without my permission again, I'll rip yours off," she says as she begins to work beside me.

"Noted." We work in tension-filled silence until it's time to clean up for lunch.

CADENCE

I swear that was the longest morning of my life. Working beside Barrick almost killed me. Every time I started a new task, he was right beside me. I really wanted him to leave me alone so I could figure out how I felt about my dad and what that kiss really meant. Now that I'm done with my lunch, I finally have a chance to breathe.

I need to talk to someone, so I call Lauren. She doesn't answer so I decide to call Jade. She's the next best thing to Lauren. She picks up after the first ring.

"Hey Cadence! What you doin'?" she questions.

"Just finished working. You busy?" I ask.

"Not really. I thought about going to the studio for a little extra practice. You wanna come?"

"Absolutely."

"I'll pick you up in twenty minutes."

I yell to Mom in the kitchen to let her know what is going on. She seems relieved to see that I'm venturing out with someone. I take a quick shower to remove the dirt from my body and slide on my dance clothes.

I grab my bag and walk outside to wait for Jade on the front porch. I'm relieved to see that Barrick is gone. I can't get him out of my mind. He's cute but he's been a pain since I got here. I don't understand him or any other guy for that matter. Speaking of other guys, I still have to text Dad back. I quickly pull out my phone and send him a one-word text. *Whatever.*

Jade is super bubbly today when she picks me up. I think I need whatever she's smoking. I'm shocked to see the parking lot is empty when we get to the studio.

"Is it okay we're here?" I question.

"Yeah, it's fine. Ms. Lyndsay will be here in a few minutes. She lets some of us older girls come in without those wild little ones running around. She really focuses on pushing us while we don't have the interruptions."

When Ms. Lyndsay arrives, we follow her into the studio. She tells us to stretch and she will be right in. We do, and as she begins to play the music my body knows what to do. My only problem is that my mind continues to wander to my dad and Barrick. They have both consumed my mind today, and I don't like it. I want to be in control, and dance is my time.

As we take a water break, Jade stops me. "Are you okay? You seem a little off."

"It's been a long morning."

"Oh I forgot you were up early working," she says as she bends down to take a sip of water.

"It's not that. Well, that's part of it but my dad texted me and pissed me off. He said he couldn't have me for Thanksgiving when he was the one that asked me to come and just said, *sorry maybe Christmas.* I just got so mad and started yelling at Barrick. And the worst part is that he made me shut up by attacking my freaking lips." Jade spews water onto the wall.

"Are you serious?" she asks.

"Yeah, and as much as I hate to admit it. I kinda liked those lips."

Jade starts to smile and before I can ask why she's smiling, Ms. Lyndsay tells us break time is over.

The next ninety minutes fly by and I've managed to tune everything out. It feels amazing. As we wrap up, Ms. Lyndsay asks to speak to both of us. She informs us that she'd like to see us do a duet, and asks if I'd be willing to show her what I had been working on. I'm unsure of how I feel about this. The routine was for Lauren and me, but I've seen Jade dance and know she'd be a great partner. She asks if we have a few more minutes and we do. I search for the music and take my spot on the floor. Jade presses play and I wait for the downbeat of "Wicked Ones." Taking a deep breath, I put everything into it. When the song ends, Jade begins to smile while Ms. Lyndsay takes a few steps toward me. *Please stay out of my personal space.* She pauses as if reading my mind.

"Cadence, that's brilliant. Did your instructor choreograph it?" she asks.

"No, I did," I say.

"I'd love to see Jade do this with you, if that's okay." I smile and Jade hurries to the floor. She watches as I begin and then follows in place. I'm amazed at how effortless it is for her, and when the music fades I realize that the two of us are better together than Lauren and me.

"Girls, I'd love to see you take this to Nationals. There's a lot of TV coverage and Cadence, I think this could be the missing piece for you. What do you girls think?" she asks, looking between the two of us.

I'd be lying if I said I was completely okay with it, but if I can't do this with Lauren, Jade is the only person I'd trust to perform it with. I look at Jade and can see the excitement on her face and then look to Ms. Lyndsay. "Sounds great."

"Okay, girls, you have a lot of work ahead of you but I know you can pull it off. Now let's go rest up," Ms. Lyndsay says.

We wait for Ms. Lyndsay to gather her bag and lock up before walking to Jade's car. We wave goodbye as Ms. Lyndsay pulls out of the lot. Getting inside, Jade turns the ignition but the car won't start. We both look at each other.

"Crap! I bet I need another starter. I swear, every time I turn 'round it's gone bad." She takes out her phone to call her dad.

"Hey! Where's Dad? Seriously?" she says to the person on the phone. "My dang car needs another starter. Can you come and help me?" she questions. "I'm going to walk to the Shake Shop and wait. Thanks," she says as she hangs up. "Help's on the way," she says, but she seems worried. "Let's go grab a drink while we wait."

We walk into the Shake Shop and Jade orders the biggest milkshake I've ever seen. "What?" she questions.

"That can't be good for you," I say, but she shrugs it off while I order an unsweetened tea and splurge on an order of fries.

"Can I have one of those?" Jade asks.

"Sure." She takes the fry and dips it in her milkshake. Gross!

"Don't look at me like that. Try it." I take a fry and I'm amazed at how the salt and sweet complement each other.

"That is good!" I say as I notice Jade's eyes flick toward the door. I glance over my shoulder and see Barrick.

"Uggggh! What's he doing here?" I sigh.

"Jade, you ready?" he asks as he approaches.

I look between them. Barrick is looking at Jade. Jade is looking at me and her eyes are as big as saucers.

"Um, he's here to pick us up. He's my brother." I believe the world just stopped spinning.

"What did you say?"

"Barrick is my b-r-o-t-h-e-r," she says as he smiles.

I take my fries and drink and toss them in the trash, having completely lost my appetite.

Our ride to Gran's feels like an eternity. I don't say much, and Barrick tries to steal glances at me in the rear view mirror. I take my phone out and text Jade.

Me: I'm going to kill you!

Jade: I'm sorry. I thought you already knew.

I don't respond to her and when I get out of the truck she gets out with me. I tell her to not waste her time, but she does anyway.

"How could you, Jade?" I yell at her.

"Every time I was going to tell you, something would happen and then it got to the point I thought you already knew."

"I told you he kissed me. I told you I liked his lips. How could you not tell me?"

"I tried to but Ms. Lyndsay called us back in the room. I'm sorry," she says as she steals a glance at Barrick before hopping in the truck.

I'm so pissed as I stand there watching them back out of the driveway. Then everything hits me at once. The day we passed him she waved and said he wasn't her type. And today when she spewed water everywhere when I told her about the kiss. That all makes sense now but why didn't anyone tell me?

I storm into the house and yell for Gran.

"What's wrong, child?" she says.

"Why didn't you tell me?" I ask her.

"You're going to have to give me more than that. What in the Sam Hill are you talkin' 'bout?" she asks.

"Barrick! He's Jade's brother."

"And…" Gran says.

"He attacked my lips this morning and I told Jade, and then her car broke down, and guess who showed up to the rescue? Barrick! Why didn't anyone tell me?"

"With all due respect, you never asked and I figured one of them would have told ya."

"Well they didn't!" I yell.

"Lower your tone, young lady. I don't know what the big deal is anyway." I just look at her because I don't even know what to say.

Mom walks down the hall. "What's wrong with her?" she asks Gran.

"Oh, Barrick kissed her and she found out he's Jade's brother."

"Oh," Mom says like it's no big deal.

"Why are you guys acting like it's no big deal? I didn't know the truth, and he *kissed me* to shut me up when I was yelling about my text from Dad."

"He did what?!" Mom exclaims.

"Yeah, dear old Dad texted me this morning and cancelled Thanksgiving. Needless to say, my mouth got the best of me and Barrick took it upon himself to shut it."

"Good for him!" Gran says as she turns to walk away and I stand there speechless.

BARRICK

"Jade! I thought you were by yourself," I say as we drive home.

"Why does it matter?" she asks. She pauses and before I can answer, she continues. "Oh wait, maybe it's because you attacked her lips this morning!"

"She told you!"

"Yeah, did you not hear her yelling about it a minute ago?" I shake my head no because I just heard yapping. "I was going to tell her but when she told me about the kiss this morning, I was afraid she'd be mad at me. I thought I'd wait until our ride home, and you can see how well that turned out," she says crossing her arms and looking out the window.

"What did she say about it?" he questions and I turn and punch him in the shoulder.

"You're such a pig! Cadence is pissed off at me because I'm related to you and you want to know if she liked it!"

"What did she say?" I question her again and smile.

"I'm not tellin'," Jade states with a grin. That tells me all I need to know, Cadence Lewis liked my lips.

"No worries Jade, your silence speaks volumes."

CADENCE

*J*ade texts and calls, but I don't answer. I'm still pissed. I try to call it an early night, but I know that when I wake up I'll have to work with Barrick. Just great! I rack my brain for a way to get back at him in the morning, but I come up short. At some point I drift off to sleep, but my mind replays our kiss over and over, but in my dreams I don't push him away.

After a fitful night's sleep, I hurry to the barn to get started when I notice that Barrick's not here. I try to hurry, but become clumsy and spill some feed.

"Let me help you," I hear him say as I sweep up the feed.

"Oh, I believe you've helped me enough," I say.

I hear his footsteps approach. "Look, I'm sorry I didn't tell you about Jade. I didn't realize it was a big deal. I know she didn't think about it either. Be pissed off at me, but not her. I can't stand to see her upset."

"What do you mean? She's the one that didn't tell me the truth."

"You're the first person she's actually herself around. I've watched my sister try and fit the Maddie mold for years. It's like the girl I've known my entire life is finally around for the world to see. Cadence, the moment you nominated her for homecoming queen changed her life. She needed someone besides me to believe in her."

I take my hand and place it on my heart. "Awe, isn't that sweet! Her big brother is sticking up for her," I say sarcastically.

"Yeah, because that's what I do. I stick up for people I care about, and you need to find someone to do the same for you."

"What is that supposed to mean?"

"Every time someone gets close to you, you push them away. I've watched it since you got here. You keep Ms. Mae, your mom, and Jade at arm's length. Just when I think you're going to wake up and lose that chip on your shoulder, it shows back up sharper than a two-edged sword."

"You've got some nerve!"

"Do I?" he asks as he walks past me and starts to work. As I continue to sweep up the feed, he's soon standing beside me again. "I thought I said I could do it my self."

"You might have said it, but I'm not going to let you. It's okay to depend on other people," he says as he starts to help me, and I mumble under my breath. For some reason, I let him help me. Once it's cleaned up, I deliver the feed and leave him alone to clean the stalls.

When I finish, I see the grossest thing ever.

"What are you doing to Daisy?" I scream at him.

Barrick looks over his shoulder. "I'm checking her. She's pregnant, remember?" I seriously think I'm going to puke.

"Don't they make ultrasounds for that?" I question.

"Yeah, but that costs money," he says as he walks to the sink and begins to apply soap and water like what he was doing was no big deal.

"That's gross!" I say as I turn and walk toward the house, but not before I hear Barrick telling me to call Jade. Just as his words leave his mouth, my phone rings. It's Jade and I reluctantly answer my phone.

"Hello," I say, unenthused.

"I'm soooooo sorry, Cadence!"

"Look, I don't need a sorry. I just need to know why you didn't tell me," I say to her.

"Honestly, every time I tried I got interrupted, but I should have told you before Barrick got there yesterday. I had hoped my dad would pick us up. Honestly, after you told me about him kissing you I was afraid you'd hate me. I know you don't want to hear an apology anymore, but I really didn't mean it."

I take a minute and think about her words. As much as I want to stay pissed at her, I can't. She's the one person that I have been able to count on. She's my dance partner, friend, and honestly the only person I know in town except for her brother. Brother? That's just so weird.

"Fine," I say.

"Really?" she says with excitement.

"Yeah. I'll see you in the morning. Oh and for the record, I still think he's a pain in my arse." She laughs and we hang up.

This is the week I should be hanging out with Lauren in New York, dancing at my studio, and taking Dad's credit card shopping on Black Friday, but I'm not. Instead, I'm stuck here working my rear off. I really thought I was getting used to being here, but I guess knowing I should have gone home this week is making life difficult. I just want a break. I want to blink my eyes and go back to a time when my family was happy. I don't care if it doesn't last. I want a tiny piece of what my life used to be like.

I thought all the physical labor would work out my anger, but I feel like it just makes it worse. Thankfully, Barrick has kept to himself and not pulled any pranks on me. I'm sure he thinks I'm mad at him but, for once, I'm not.

BARRICK

Cadence has been helping more at the barn with school being out and
I've been keeping my distance. I know she's angry and I don't want to
make things worse. I haven't even pranked her this week.

She's huffing and puffing as she cleans out one of the stalls.

"Hey Cadence, feel free to take a break if you need one," I say.

"What?" she asks, finally looking at me.

"I said, take a break. You've been working hard all morning."

"Fine," she says, throwing the shovel. I take a step to follow her, but
stop myself. I think she's made it pretty clear that she doesn't want
any help from me. Within a few minutes I hear music coming from
outside the barn, I try to refrain from going to watch, but it's
impossible.

As I hear the barn door slide open, I turn and am caught by
Ms. Mae.

"Boy whatcha doin'?" she questions.

"I heard music and decided to check it out."

"That so. Well, let me throw this out there for ya." I turn and give
her my full attention. "Cadence isn't a girl I'd sneak up on. I thought
you knew that already," she says.

"I know, but..."

"Don't but me. I know you like her, but she's got some stuff to
work out."

"I don't," I reply as she places her hands on her hips like she doesn't
believe me. "Ms. Mae, she's pissed about something and for once it's
not because of me. I just feel bad for her."

"Don't pity her, but be there for her. She's dealing with more than
any teenage girl should have to. Now, get back to work."

"Yes ma'am," I answer. When Ms. Mae leaves, I quickly finish my
tasks and try to think of a way to cheer Cadence up. I get an idea but
I'm unsure if it will work, so I text Jade to run my plan by her. She's a
little cautious, but says that anything is worth a try.

When I hear the music fade, I slide the door open and walk out to
talk to Cadence.

"Um, Cadence you got a minute?" She looks at me like I'm crazy.

"I've got all the time in the world," she says, tossing her arms in the air.

"What do you say we get outta here?"

"What do you mean?" she asks suspiciously.

"I've got an idea but I need you to trust me."

"No, I'm good," she says as she starts to walk off.

"I ran it by Jade and she said she thinks you'll like it." She stops in her tracks and turns around. "Go get ready. I'm going to run home. I'll be back."

"Okay… can you give me a hint?"

"No, just be ready to have a good time. I'll be back in an hour."

CADENCE

*W*hat was that all about? Barrick has been overly nice to me today and when I think about it, he has been nice all week. I take my phone out and call Jade.

"Girl, what is your brother up to?"

"Look, trust me on this. You'll have fun."

"Seriously? That's all you're going to give me?" I ask.

"Yeah, and be nice. He doesn't do stuff like this often."

"You're going too, right?" I confirm.

"Nope. Aaron and I already had plans."

I hang up with Jade and call for Mom to come to my room.

"Mom, I'm going out. I don't know where, but Barrick just demanded that I get ready. He'll be back in an hour. Do you know anything?" I question.

Mom stands there and looks at me. "I have no clue. Mom! Come in here!" she yells. Oh my gosh! I don't need the entire peanut gallery in my business.

"Mom, Barrick asked Cadence out."

"'Bout time," Gran says with a smirk.

"He did not!" I exclaim as they both turn to look at me. "He told me to go get ready and he'd be back in an hour. That is not how you ask a girl out on a date. I just wanted to know if you knew what he was up to?" I say to them.

They both shake their heads no as Gran takes a step toward me. "Barrick's a good boy. He sees good in everyone, and I've watched how he looks at you. He sees what your mama and I know is in here," she says, pointing to my heart. "I also think he knows you've got a bigger problem. Maybe he wants you to have fun 'cause we all know you never go out. Have fun, but be careful," she says as she pulls me into her arms.

"Cadence, you might want to hurry up. The clock's ticking and I know you," Mom says with a laugh.

"Couldn't you at least tell me what to wear," I yell after them. I just hear them giggle as I turn to my closet to find something to wear.

He left me no clues about what we were doing. The air is chilly at night, but not like home. I finally decide on leggings and a long top. I pull out my designer boots that stop just above the ankle. Straightening my hair, I look in the mirror. I look exhausted and sad. Maybe they are right. Maybe I need to have some fun, but I wish I could have fun in New York, not Delight.

———

BARRICK

Jade is waiting for me when I get home.

"So she's already called me and is totally confused about what is going on. I mean. I think she'll have fun, but she's not a girl from 'round here. Take it easy on her."

"What do you mean?"

"It means take her to do something you know she'll like then go ahead with your plans if there's time. Not to mention, she's not going to be dressed for it. It rained this week."

"I didn't think about that." Then it dawns on me, I've got one more stop before I pick her up.

"Can I ask you something, Bare? Why do you feel like you have to do this? I mean, she's my friend not yours."

"Jade, since the day she walked into the barn I knew she was different, but there's something in her soul that's hurting. I have no clue what it is, but today she was furious. She's always got an attitude with me, but this was different. For the first time, her irritation wasn't aimed at me, or the farm, and it really bothered me. No one should have to keep that inside."

"I know."

"What do you mean? You agree or you know what she's pissed about?" I ask, fishing for details.

"I'm not sure I know exactly, but I think it has to do with her dad. She's mentioned him to me, but never goes into details."

"Yeah, well the way she went off after getting a text today tells me something definitely ain't right. I better get ready. Thanks, Jade."

"No problem. Oh, and please don't kiss her! You're liable to be six feet under," she giggles.

After I shower, I slide on a pair of clean jeans and a button up. I grab boots and my hat from the closet. I slide the hat on my head and look in the mirror, then I take it off and leave it on my dresser as I walk out of the room.

As I walk downstairs, I hear Jade whistle. "Stop it," I say to her.

"Where's your cap? You never leave home without it, not even on Sundays," she says.

"Very funny," I say to her as Mom enters the room.

"Barrick, you look nice. Where are you goin'?" Mom asks.

"I'm taking Ms. Mae's granddaughter out, but it's not a date," I say sternly because I know Mom will eat this up.

"Oh, okay. Be careful, and don't forget that we're eating at Memaw's tomorrow for Thanksgiving around two."

"Yes ma'am," I say as I hug her and walk to my truck. Looking at my clock, I know that it's going to be cutting it close, but the feed store isn't far.

When I get to the store, I find exactly what I'm looking for. My only concern is the size. I quickly text Jade and she is able to help me out. She then requests to see what patterns are available. I send her a quick picture, but don't wait for her response. I quickly pay the cashier, who looks at me funny, and I hide them in my backseat.

Arriving at Ms. Mae's, I debate whether I should wait in the truck or pick her up at the door. I decide that even though this isn't a date, I'm still a southern gentleman and Cadence needs to see how country boys do things.

Just before I knock on the door, it flies open. "Let's go," she says as she hurries out the door and pulls it shut behind her. So much for that idea. I manage to open the truck door for her and help her in. Once we're both settled in the truck, I take a look at her. She's absolutely stunning, and I wonder if the outfit cost more than my paycheck.

"Are we going to go or what?" she snaps.

"Yeah. You okay? You kinda ran outta the house."

"I'm fine. I just don't want Mom and Gran to get the wrong idea."

"What might that be?" I ask for kicks.

She cuts her eyes at me like a knife. "Like a date."

"Yeah, this isn't a date."

I turn onto the main road and drive toward Asheville. I park downtown where all the shops are located. Cadence opens her door and looks around.

"I thought you might want to check out some of the galleries and shops. Jade loves to come here, and they have some pretty awesome restaurants."

"Oh, it's very different than Delight," she says as she walks next to me.

"That's for sure. It's a decent-sized town, but not as big as where you're from I'm sure."

"True," she says as the sun beams down and warms the cool air. We walk toward the first store, and I follow wherever she leads.

CADENCE

I'm absolutely blown away by the art that I've seen, but I'm even more amazed that Barrick thought to bring me here. It's almost as if they've taken a fancy exhibit from New York, broken it down into segments, and placed it in different stores. I take my time admiring the works and trace my fingers over some.

As my stomach begins to rumble, I hear him laugh. "You hungry?" he asks.

"Yeah, I kinda skipped lunch," I reply.

"Me too. Come on," Barrick says as he places his hand on the small of my back and guides me toward a side street. Walking down the road, I see several restaurants, and as we approach The Lobster Trap he pauses. "How's this?" he questions.

"It's fine," I say and see an uneasiness cross his brow.

Once we are seated, Barrick tells me all his favorite meals. I skim the menu and know exactly what I want—a steam bowl.

Barrick asks me questions and keeps the conversation moving as we wait for our food. When the food arrives, we stop talking and eat, and as we finish Barrick asks if I want dessert. I tell him no, but I would love to stop by the bakery. I can't turn down a freshly baked croissant. Barrick insists on paying for our dinner. He keeps telling me that's what guys around here do. Well, I think that's ridiculous. I'm very capable of taking care of myself.

Once again, Barrick holds the door open for me when we get to the bakery. It's kind of nice, but strange. It feels like something out of an old movie. Walking to the counter, I'm in heaven. I take out my purse and grab my debit card. Glancing in his direction, I ask him if he wants anything, and when he tries to pay for it, I tell him this is the least I can do. I'm amazed when he actually lets me win this battle.

"I'd like to mix a dozen." Barrick looks at me like I'm crazy. I turn toward him. "A good croissant is hard to find, and I'm sure Gran and Mom will want one, too."

"You know you're going to have to hide those in your room," he says with a laugh, and I elbow him as I tell the cashier I'd also like a maple bacon cupcake for Barrick. Yuck!

As we walk out the door, Barrick holds it open again and I waste no time opening the box to try a chocolate drizzle croissant.

"Hmmmm," I say.

"Good?" he questions with a smile.

"Yeah, you want to try it?" I say offering it to him, and when he takes a big hunk out of it, I gasp. "I meant tear a piece off," I say in disgust.

"Sorry. You were waving it around at my face so I thought you were sharing," he says with a shrug.

We walk back to his truck, and I have to say Barrick Carpenter has turned my terrible day into a sweet one... or maybe it was the croissant.

BARRICK

We leave Asheville for our final destination. We sit in silence and listen to the music playing through the speakers. As we get closer, I'm unsure if I made the right decision. She's not a country girl and this is definitely not something that happens all the time. I decide to go for it as I turn down a two-lane road. She looks at me with concern.

"You're not taking me out to the middle of nowhere to kill me, are you?" she says in a serious tone and then gives me a half grin.

"No, but we are going somewhere else. Have you ever been on a hayride?" I ask her.

"No, well not unless you call riding on the Gator one." I shake my head no. "Barrick, I appreciate it, but I don't think it's my thing."

"How do you know? You've never been." There's no way I'm turning around. I haven't been out here in years and Jade swore it was a good idea. She doesn't answer and I continue to drive in silence until we see a sign for the farm.

"I thought you said a hayride. That's a sign for a pumpkin patch. Halloween was last month."

"Yeah, but they continue to do hayrides and a corn maze through the end of November. I promise it will be fun. You can actually enjoy the country life without having to work on the farm."

We turn down a muddy dirt road and I can see the horror flash on her face.

"Um Barrick, I am not getting out in that. You can turn around now." I pull my truck into the makeshift parking lot and turn off the engine. "Did you not hear me?" she snips.

"I did, but I'm prepared."

"What do you mean *prepared*?"

"Hold on a sec." I reach behind my seat and tell her to close her eyes. She is reluctant, but finally listens. I take the pair of paisley print galoshes and set them on top of the console.

"Can I open them now?"

"Yeah." I'm terrified as I wait for her reaction. The fashion queen herself is either going to love or hate my gesture.

"You got me rain boots?"

"Yeah, I knew it was kinda nasty out here, and thought you wouldn't want to mess up those expensive shoes you have on. I also notice that Ms. Mae's shoes are a few sizes too big, and I knew you wouldn't spend your money on something like this."

"They're paisley," she says as she turns up her nose.

"It was either that or chevron and from what I've heard, that's as bad as monogramming everything," I say.

"Good point and smart choice," she says with a smile. "Do you really think they'll fit?"

"They should," I say as she slides them on. "Well, what do you think?"

"They fit, but they feel so weird."

"Well, let's go try them out," I say as I help her down from the truck.

29

CADENCE

*H*oly crap! I'm not one to get random acts of kindness from people, but I have to say Barrick has blown my mind today. The kindness he has shown is pretty awesome considering I haven't been very nice to him and even yelled at him for something that wasn't even his fault. I lumped him in with my dad and it wasn't fair.

He helps me down from the truck and into the mushy grass. I'm so glad he bought me the boots so I didn't ruin the ones I had on. He really can be a sweet guy. We walk to the entrance and make our way around to the different activities while we wait to line up for the next ride. I'm amazed that there is so much you can do with corn. I thought we ate it, but apparently, you can make a sandbox, shoot it like a torpedo, and play a bean bag toss game with it that Barrick quickly informs me is called cornhole. He attempts to show me how it's done and when his bag makes it in the hole, my competitiveness gets the best of me. He tries to show me what to do, but I quickly pull my arm from his and do it myself. When the bag lands far left, he gives me an I-told-you-so look. I try it again and land on the board. I jump up and down and laugh at him but he quickly informs me he's still winning.

We don't get to finish the game before it's time for the ride. Barrick points to a table where there are pots of hot chocolate and apple cider. I'm not a hot chocolate fan so I vote for the cider. We take our drinks and walk up the makeshift steps to the back of a trailer filled with hay. Barrick takes a seat and I sit beside him. After the seats are completely filled, the driver tells us the history of the farm. As the engine roars, it's hard to hear what Barrick is saying to me. He must realize it so he moves in closer and that's when the hot cider spills all over my clothes.

"Oh crap." I yell and everyone looks at me like I'm insane.

"Cadence, are you okay?" he questions and looks apologetically toward a mother covering her child's ears.

"I'm fine," I say bitterly, but as I glance toward the cute little girl I change my tune. "I'm okay but it was hot and it startled me. Ma'am, I'm sorry for my language. I didn't expect for that to happen." She tells me it's okay, and Barrick smiles at me.

"I'm sorry that happened, but thank you for not going all yankee on me," he says with a laugh and I can't do anything but smile.

As we arrive back at the starting point, Barrick leans in to me. "Are you sure you're okay?" he asks with concern.

"I'm fine, just wet and my legs are freezing, not to mention these jeans cost a fortune, but it should come out in the wash."

"Well, let's get you home and cleaned up."

Barrick takes my hand and guides me down the steps. When my feet hit the ground, I'm surprised when Barrick doesn't let go of my hand. It's thoughtful and sweet, but I can't resist saying something. When I'm about to open my mouth, he lets go and I let the words evaporate into thin air.

Our ride back to Gran's doesn't take as long as I had expected. Barrick and I talk a lot, and he points out different places and a million different deer. I swear they are everywhere. That's when he informs me that I'm going to have to increase my time at the barn so he can hunt. I quickly shoot that idea down with dance competitions about to start, and he says he at least had to try.

As we get back to Gran's, I'm kind of sad to see the night end. I hate to admit it but Barrick and I had a great time, and it was nice to get away from here. He might not be as bad as I thought.

"Thanks," I say as I begin to pull the handle on the truck door.

"You're very welcome. I'm glad we went," he says and I smile because I am too. "You know if you ever need to get away again, just holler."

"I will," I say as I step out and begin to walk toward the house with my new galoshes in my hands. As I reach the step, I hear Barrick call my name, and I see him walking toward me with a box. *How could I have forgotten those?* I set the shoes on the steps and walk to meet him halfway.

"I figured I'd be a dead man if I took these home," he says with a laugh.

"Yeah you would. You sure you don't want one?" I ask him.

"Nah, but maybe tomorrow. I had a great time," he says and starts to walk away.

"Hey Barrick!" He turns and I take a step toward him and quickly place a swift kiss on his cheek. "Thank you for a great night," I say and then walk to the house.

Walking into the kitchen I yell for Mom and Gran, "I've got croissants!"

Mom and Gran are there within minutes. "Where did you get these?" Gran questions.

"We went to Asheville," I state.

"Oooooh," she says as she takes a bite. "This is amazing. Regina, taste one," she says and Mom does as we all sit around the kitchen table.

"So how was your non-date?" Mom asks.

"Good," I say, trying to hide a smile.

"I see that smile. He's not so bad after all, is he?" Gran smirks as I shrug my shoulders.

BARRICK

She kissed my cheek. I know it was on the cheek, but she's never this nice to me. As I pull up to my house, I can see Jade is bundled up on the front porch reading a book waiting for me. When my headlights come into view, she puts her book down and I know I have to tell her everything.

"How was it?" she questions.

"It was fun," I say, trying to go in the house.

"Are you kiddin' me? I let you go off with my friend, who I know you have the hots for, and you tell me it was fun?" she fires at me.

"Jade, we had a really good time," I say with a smile.

Jade covers her mouth with her hands and gasps. "You kissed her didn't you!" I shake my head no. "Then why you got that grin all over your face?"

"Maybe cause we had a good time, that's all."

"If you say so, but you know she'll tell me everything."

"Well, there's not much to tell," I say as I go in the house.

CADENCE

The moment Mom and Gran leave me alone, I go upstairs to call Lauren. She answers on the second ring.

"Hey! You're not going to believe my—" I start to say but Lauren cuts me off.

"Ohmygosh! I got an audition for the NYC Ballet! Can you believe it?"

"That's awesome," I say, genuinely excited for her. She proceeds to tell me everything about the audition and what's been going on at the studio and school. Before I know it she's disconnected the phone and has no clue about what is going on in my world. Looks like I'll have to tell her about my non-date with Barrick some other time.

30

CADENCE

*T*hanksgiving morning I roll out of bed and get ready to go to the barn, but today I'm not wearing Gran's boots. I have my own pair that fit.

"Look at those snazzy shoes!" Gran says.

"Yeah, Barrick got them for me. It was either these or chevron. Thank goodness they aren't chevron," I laugh as I grab a cup of yogurt before going to help at the barn.

I see Barrick's truck and smile as I walk out to the barn. As I slide open the door, I'm shocked to see that Jade is with him too.

"What are you doing here?" I question.

"Aw, ya know, nothing to do on this Thanksgiving Day." I can see right through her. "Okay, maybe because I haven't seen ya, I thought I'd come help too," she says. "And, maybe get more information out of you than I got from Barrick last night about the non-date. I can't believe you didn't call me when you got home."

I realize I called Lauren first and she didn't even care. I should have called Jade. At least I know I can count on her. I notice how comfortable she is around everything in here. It's like this is normal.

"So I take it you've done this before?" I ask.

"Yeah, but y'all got fancy equipment. We only have a few cows to milk at home so we have to use our hands." I crinkle my nose as she talks about it. "You should try it one time."

"You're kidding, right?" I ask, as she shakes her head no.

"Come on. I'll show you," she says and for some reason I follow. Maybe because I know she's not going to prank me like Barrick.

Jade takes a seat on a stool and wraps her hands around those udders like it's a natural thing. I'm starting to squirm just thinking about it. She starts to move her hands a certain way and then bam, milk appears. She gives me a quick lesson and then says it's my turn. It takes me a few minutes and I ask if I can wear gloves. They both laugh at me and tell me no. Taking a deep breath, I go for it, and I've got nothing.

"You want some help?" Barrick asks.

"Nope," I say as he shakes his head and walks away. Jade walks over to me and bends down to help me. I'm freaking milking a cow. How crazy is that?

"Hey, you know what?" Jade whispers.

"What, and why are we whispering?" I question.

"I've got an idea," she says and then quickly tells me in my ear. I'm so game.

"Hey Barrick! She's given in. Can you come help her?" Jade yells.

"Yeah, hold on," he says and we try to refrain from laughing.

Jade takes a step back and Barrick squats down beside me giving me instructions. I play stupid, and when he leans in to help me, I squirt milk right in his face. It startles him and we begin to laugh.

Wiping it away, he looks at both of us. "Cadence, we had a truce," he says and I smile.

"It was your sister's idea. Not mine," I say to him.

"That so?" he says, looking at Jade.

"Yup," she says with a huge grin as he turns to walk away, telling her to sleep with one eye open tonight.

"Cadence, that was hilarious! So whatcha think?" she asks pointing to the cow.

"It was weird, but not many people I know can say they've done it," I reply.

"True. Come on, let's hook them up so we can get ready for some food."

We finish up this morning and Jade tells me they are going to their memaw's for Thanksgiving. Barrick tells me he'll be back for his duties this afternoon. I tell him Mom, Gran, and I can handle it. Let's face it; he does more than his share, and today is a day of giving. They leave and I walk to the house only to be scared to death by Gran.

"So you told him to take the afternoon off?" Gran inquires without a smile.

"Yeah. Was that not okay?" I question.

"That's my job, but I'll let it slide because I was going to tell him that anyways," she says with a smile. "So tell me, what made you make that decision?"

I ponder on it for a moment. "I guess because Jade was talking about going to their memaw's. I just felt bad for him to have to come back over here and be away from his family."

"And that, Cade, is the perfect answer," she says as she tosses her arm around my shoulder. "You want to help me get ready for our Thanksgiving feast?"

"Why not?" I say.

"You might want to shower first," Gran says, wrinkling her nose.

After my shower, I find Mom and Gran in the kitchen in aprons and working hard. I can't comprehend why the three of us need all of this food. I think about asking, but then Gran starts giving orders and I follow.

As I'm finishing the pecan pie, my cellphone begins to ring. I quickly wipe my hands and see that it's Dad.

"Hello?" I answer as I walk out to the back porch.

"Hey, Cade. I wanted to call and wish you Happy Thanksgiving."

"Thanks, Dad. What are you doing today?" I ask knowing that's a loaded question.

"Mindy and I are going to her parents."

"Oh." It's the only word I can manage because now I know why he didn't want me to come. He had other plans that don't include his old family.

"How are you?" he asks.

"I'm hanging in there. Life here isn't so bad," I tell him as I try to refrain from showing my true emotions.

"See, I told you it would all work out. Well, I've got to go, but keep your eyes on the mail. I've sent you something," he says. I want to be excited because Dad used to give me great gifts, but knowing he'd rather be with *her* family and not me makes me sad. Hanging up, I walk back inside to see that Mom and Gran are staring at me.

"What?" I say as I walk back to my pie and pick it up to place it in the oven. They look at each other and shrug their shoulders. I do my best to shake off the sadness, but it's no use and everything seems to go to fall apart the rest of the afternoon. I burned my pie, got cranberry salad on my white shirt, and when we went to work at the barn that afternoon not only did I step in poop a cow splattered poop all over me while I was removing the cups. Happy Thanksgiving to me.

BARRICK

My family and I make the short trip to my memaw's. When we arrive, Jade and I help our parents carry in food and then go out back where all of our cousins are setting up for the annual flag football game.

We start the game and have an awesome afternoon. At halftime, Memaw yells for us to come and eat. It happens every year like clockwork. After stuffing ourselves silly, we take a break and watch football on TV. My mind wanders to Ms. Mae and Cadence and I hope they are enjoying their day. When Jade leaves her phone unattended, I swipe it and get Cadence's number.

"What are you doing with my phone?" Jade asks.

"Being nosey like any good brother would be," I say.

"Right!" she says as if she can read my mind. "All you had to do was ask."

"Ask what?" my cousin questions.

"Oh, he's got the hots for my friend Cadence. Not to mention he works for her grandma," Jade says, completely sure of herself, and the entire room starts to laugh.

"I don't know how you put up with her," my younger cousin Jude says.

"It's rough. I'll tell y'all that," I say and look at Jade like I'm going to kill her. Now the question is do I call or not. Maybe I'll just hold on to it for future reference.

After we let our food settle, we finish our game outside and as the afternoon sky begins to fade, we say our goodbyes and go home.

CHRISTMAS

CADENCE

*J*t's been three weeks since Thanksgiving and I haven't gotten anything from Dad. *Maybe he lied or maybe it's going to be something extra special on Christmas? What if he's coming to see me? No, that can't be it.* I'm beginning to get irritated and Jade has been asking me what is going on. I can honestly say she's become the one person I turn to, but then there's also Barrick. Since the day he took me to Asheville, things have been different. I know he likes me because let's face it, I'm pretty fabulous, but it's something else. I catch him watching me when we're working and I don't find it creepy. I've told myself over and over that I don't need a guy or want one, but if I had to right now, I'd choose him. But he doesn't need to know that.

Now that Christmas break has arrived, I'm stoked. It means no homework but I still have my farm work and dance. I'm not thrilled about the work, but dance gets me through the day.

As Barrick and I finish in the stalls Monday morning, I see the mail truck stop at the end of the road and the mailman place a big envelope in the mailbox. I wonder if it's for me. I don't tell Barrick where I'm going and hurry to the end of the drive. I soon realize I should have taken the Gator.

Opening the mailbox, I find sales ads and an envelope addressed to me. *Funny. It's not from Dad. It's not his handwriting.* I take it and open the envelope. I see that there is a plane ticket dated for the day after Christmas. I pull the Christmas card out, and when I read the sweet note, inside my insides tighten into a ball. She wrote it. It's *her* handwriting. *Couldn't he have a least written it himself?* I want to throw it on the ground, but think twice. I've wanted to go back to New York since I left, but I'm not going to play nice when I get there.

BARRICK

Where did she go? I stop what I'm doing and walk to the doorway to see her standing at the mailbox. It takes all of two seconds to see her happiness fade and all I can make out is her moving her hands and obviously yelling about something.

As she starts to walk back, I walk back inside and finish up. "So you got any matches?" she asks, catching me off guard.

"Sorry, I don't smoke," I say.

"Me neither, but I've got some stuff I want to get rid of. Can you help me?" she asks. I can't tell her no because she looks like she's ready to kill someone.

"Sure. This doesn't involve a dead body, does it?" I ask, trying to make her laugh. She doesn't find it funny. "I'm kidding. Whatcha got?" I ask, pointing to the mail.

"Oh a flight to New York," she says with a fake smile.

"Shouldn't you be happy about that?"

"I should, but it's who sent it that pisses me off." I don't say anything and walk to the closet and rummage around for matches. *Bingo.*

"I got matches. What are we burning?"

"Everything but the ticket," she says and we walk toward a metal barrel full of wood that I've been meaning to burn. I take some straw and light it first to get it going. "You want to talk about it?" I ask, but she doesn't say anything as she takes everything but the flight ticket and tosses it in the fire.

"Did you know my dad couldn't even write me a Christmas card?" she asks as she watches it burn. I have no idea what to say. "Instead, he had that home-wrecking bimbo do it."

"I'm sorry," I say to her and she snaps.

"Sorry? Why re you sorry, Barrick? You didn't do anything wrong. Do you think sorry fixes everything? Cause, guess what? It doesn't!" she yells at me, and I don't know what to do. Instead of speaking, I take a step toward her and wrap my arms around her. She tries to pull away, but I tighten them more and she does the thing I least expected; she begins to cry. I don't say anything. I hold her and let her know I'm here for her. I have no idea what it's like not having both parents at home, but to know that her dad doesn't treat her the way she should be treated makes my heart hurt. I know that from this point on, I'm going to make her feel loved whether she likes it or not.

32

CADENCE

I broke down in Barrick's arms. That is not like me. I don't need a man to fix my problems. I do my best to remove that moment from my mind, but it consumes me. I've done everything I can think of to try and forget and I've been dodging questions from Mom right and left. I know she already knows about the flight because she's hinted at it, but I don't want to talk about it. Instead, I want to enjoy Christmas with her and Gran before I fly home. The only problem is I don't want to go alone.

It's finally Christmas Eve and I'm super excited. This has always been my favorite holiday. Growing up, I loved having my mom read the Christmas story to me and then baking cookies together for Santa. So, of course, we did both today.

After dinner, we are sitting by the fireplace watching Christmas movies when there is a knock at the door. I get up and am surprised to see Barrick.

"Hey, everything okay?" I ask him.

"Yeah, Mom wanted me to drop this off to Ms. Mae," he says, holding a box.

"She's in the living room. You can take it to her." Barrick walks in as I close the door behind him. It's obvious he's been somewhere nice. He has on a pair of fancy jeans and a nice button down shirt with a pair of boots that look new.

"My, don't you look spiffy. Hot date?" Gran questions.

"No, ma'am. Just dropping this off for Mom," he says, extending the box to her.

"Well, she didn't have to do that," she says as she opens it to find a freshly baked cake. Gran pinches off a bite to taste it. "Hm, apple cake, my favorite. Y'all want some?" she asks all of us. I shake my head no, but Mom does. She looks at Barrick, who says he's good. Gran and Mom walk to the kitchen, leaving us alone.

"Is that *Holiday in Handcuffs*?" Barrick asks, looking at the TV.

"Yeah, but more importantly why do you know that?" I question.

"I have a sister who loves these awful movies. I swear every time it comes on she forces me to watch it with her."

"That so? So you want me to force you to watch it here instead? Ya know, to save you from Jade?" I ask him.

"You wouldn't have to force me," he says and my heart skips a beat as Mom and Gran enter. "I guess I'm going to run. I hope Santa's good to y'all," he says and I show him to the door.

"I hope you have a Merry Christmas," I tell him.

"I hope your Christmas is everything you want it to be," he replies.

He turns to walk down the steps but pauses. "When do you come back from New York?"

"I leave the twenty-sixth, but I'll be back New Year's Eve. Why?"

"There's always a big New Year's Eve party at The Loft. I didn't know if Jade told you or not."

"No, she hasn't."

"I know Aaron asked if she wanted to go with him, and I thought maybe if you were home that we could go together."

"I think we could do that," I say with a sweet smile. "So is this a date, Mr. Carpenter?"

"I think so," he says with a wink before he turns and walks toward his truck.

Closing the door, I turn and lean my back against it. Barrick asked me out and I totally wanted him to. Now I just have to get through this trip to New York. *What in the world? Get through? I couldn't wait to get back to New York.*

I walk into the living room and take a seat while Mom and Gran stare me down. "What?" I question.

"Care to explain why you look like a lovesick goofball?" Gran says with a mouthful of cake.

"I have no idea what you're talking about," I say as I focus back on the TV.

***

BARRICK

When I get home everyone is in the living room watching *Holiday in Handcuffs*. I should have stayed to watch it with Cadence. I try to sneak by and go to my room, but I'm not that lucky.

"Barrick, how was Ms. Mae? Did she like it?" Mom questions as I walk by the entranceway.

"She did and of course she had to sample it as soon as she opened the box," I say, trying to ease my way down the hall.

"Where do you think you're going? Don't you see what's on?" Jade asks.

"Please don't make me, Jade," I plead.

"You know the drill, bro," she says as she pats the couch. *I should have taken Cadence up on that offer. I'd much rather be sitting next to her.*

When Mom leaves the two of us alone during the commercial, Jade decides to drill me.

"So did you ask her?"

"Yes," I say, purposely not elaborating.

"Well…"

"She doesn't come home until New Year's Eve," I say, trying to play it off.

"Does that mean she said yes or no?" she questions, getting impatient.

"She said yes."

"I knew it! Oh! Why don't we pick her up from the airport? Maybe we can go eat somewhere fancy in Charlotte?" she suggests and I roll my eyes.

"Jade, I don't think I need to look that desperate. Besides, I'm sure when she gets back she's going to want to see her mom."

"What do you mean?" I know right then that I've stuck my foot in my mouth.

"Nothing. I mean, wouldn't you?" Jade looks at me like she's not buying it. "What?"

"Spill it."

"No, that's for her to tell. Let's just say her dad's not Dad of the Year."

Jade drops it and I watch the movie with her. Thankfully it's near the end. When it's over, we get the Miller High Life and oatmeal raisin cookies ready for Dad, I mean Santa.

As I lay in bed, I can't fall asleep. Cadence said yes to New Year's. I was so nervous. I've never been nervous asking a girl out before. This girl definitely has my mind messed up. She's either mad, crying, or kissing me. She definitely keeps me on my toes and I love that about her.

33

CADENCE

*I*t's Christmas morning and when I wake, I grab my cellphone and glance at the clock. It's eight-thirty! I jump out of bed and run downstairs to find that no one is in the house. Strange. I slide on boots and walk toward the barn. Sliding the door open, I see Mom and Gran milking. I kind of wish Barrick was here this morning.

"You guys didn't wake me up!" I say, walking over to them.

"You never get to sleep in and we thought that would be a good Christmas present," Mom says.

"Yeah, you deserve it. You've come a long way," Gran says.

"Well, then, I'm going back to the house." I hurry back inside and stop to see what Santa brought me. I'm surprised when I don't see much of anything. *What in the world?* I decide to peek in my stocking and find an iTunes gift card and new makeup. I know that's not why we celebrate, but a gift card and makeup? Maybe Mom and Gran are still hiding some presents until they get done in the barn. I go to the kitchen to pour a cup of coffee and suddenly hear a horn blowing. I turn to look out the window and see a Range Rover coming down the driveway with Jade's car behind it. I'm so confused.

With my cup of coffee in hand, I walk to the front porch and see that Mom and Gran are walking toward me. Barrick gets out of the Range Rover. *Oh crap! I haven't put any makeup on or brushed my hair.* I quickly set my coffee down and pull my hair in a messy bun.

"What do you think?" Mom asks.

"What do you mean? Are you selling the Suburban?" I question.

"No. It's for you. Merry Christmas," Mom cheers.

"Really? Really-Really?" I ask as she eagerly nods her head yes.

"Gran and I have been talking about it for a while so when I spoke to your dad a few weeks ago he looked into it and had it shipped here."

"Oh," I say with less enthusiasm.

"You don't like it?" Mom questions.

"I love it," I say.

"Don't you want to go check it out?" Mom asks. I'm still in shock as I walk toward the Range Rover.

"Merry Christmas," Barrick says as he hops out of the truck with a big grin on his face.

"Merry Christmas!" I hear Jade yell as she approaches the vehicle.

"Merry Christmas!" I say to both of them. "I'm going to kill you, you know," I say, looking at Barrick.

"Why? Your mom and Ms. Mae made me do it."

Barrick moves out of the way and lets me sit in the driver's seat. The seats are black leather and it has everything I could have imagined.

"You guys want to go for a ride?" I ask everyone.

"Y'all go on. Your mom and I have a few things to finish up," Gran says.

I hop in the driver's seat and Jade grabs shotgun. Barrick sits behind me. "Where to?" I ask.

"Wherever you want to go."

We take it out on the two-lane road and drive through town. I absolutely love how it handles and it fits me perfectly. There's no way

I would want to drive a truck permanently and a car doesn't seem to fit me either. I think this SUV is perfect.

When we get back to the house I wish them a Merry Christmas and thank them for helping with my gift. I tell Jade I'll call her later. I know I'll see Barrick in the morning before I leave. Mom and Gran are sitting at the kitchen table when I walk in the house, so I sit and we enjoy breakfast together and then open presents. When we finish, Mom informs me I should probably call Dad. *Great. Bah humbug.*

I grab my phone and walk to my room. "Merry Christmas, Dad," I say when he answers.

"Merry Christmas."

"I love my SUV."

"I'm glad. Did it have everything you wanted?"

"I guess, and more I'm sure. I haven't had time to check it all out," I say.

"Great. So, your flight arrives at one tomorrow. I'll make sure Mindy is there to pick you up. I've got a meeting until three, then we have a party at the Moore's tomorrow night."

"Can I get Lauren to pick me up?" I question him.

"No, I'd rather Mindy pick you up. You need to spend some time together. I think she's got a few things lined up for you two." *Great, an afternoon with the home-wrecker.* "Can I speak to your mom for a minute?" he asks, which is unusual.

"Sure." I take the phone to Mom and she walks into another room. When she returns, she hands me the phone and I say my goodbye to Dad. Mom looks like it was nothing big, and typically I can tell when he's said something to piss her off. Maybe he was being cordial and wishing her a Merry Christmas. At least that's what I hope.

We spend the remainder of the day enjoying each other's company, and when the afternoon rolls around the three of us finish the chores in record time. In my few short months here I've realized that having a farm is a huge responsibility. You never get a day off.

As the evening rolls in, we enjoy a dinner that's not your typical Christmas meal. Instead Gran steams oysters. They aren't my favorite, but they have both insisted that this is our new tradition.

Gran pulls the bucket from the water and lays them on newspaper while Mom and I take the shuckers and pry them open. I try one and almost gag.

"I can't do this," I say as I remove the slimy mess from my mouth.

"Cade, either cover it in cocktail sauce or smother it in melted butter. Either will do the trick." I shake my head as I watch Gran slurp them down.

"I think I'll just have a salad and baked potato," I say to Mom.

"Suit yourself," Gran chimes in.

When we finish eating, we all clean up together and then Mom excuses me to go pack. I grab my suitcase and stare at my closet. I decide to pack everyday clothes as well as a few fancier outfits. As I'm folding my last piece, my phone rings and it's Lauren.

"Merry Christmas, ho!" she yells.

"Back at ya," I say and we start to laugh.

"So you want me to pick you up tomorrow?" Lauren questions.

"I wish, but Bimbo has our day planned out. Dad insisted that she pick me up."

"Are you serious?"

"Yeah. And, get this, tomorrow night I have to go to a party at the Moore's. Please tell me that you are going too."

"Of course! Do you think I'd miss getting a glimpse of Jack Moore in a suit? Um no!" I smile because that is a very fine sight. We spend a few more minutes talking about what we got for Christmas and I tell her about my new car.

Before we hang up, I tell her I'll text her once I know what is going on. I can't wait to see her. I look through my suitcase again and decide to throw in my dance stuff as well. I think a little time in my old studio would be perfect.

BARRICK

Jade and I spend the afternoon with Mom and Dad and Memaw comes over to see what Santa brought like she has since we were born. I, however, can't stop thinking about Cadence standing there looking absolutely stunning in her pajamas with no makeup and her hair pulled up in one of those bird's nest-looking things. I swear she doesn't know how beautiful she is. Don't get me wrong she looks stunning when she has herself put together, but there's something about seeing her so natural.

"Hey, loverboy, snap out of it," Jade says.

"What are you talkin' 'bout?" I question.

"You've been somewhere else all day."

"No I haven't," I reply.

"Yes, you have. Ever since you saw Cadence this morning you've been all goo-goo eyed."

"Shut up," I say to her and leave the room.

When I return, Jade continues the conversation. I tell her to leave me alone, and eventually she does. However, this isn't before Memaw, Mom and Dad have started twenty questions as well.

We eat supper together and enjoy a night of Christmas movies. When everyone can't keep their eyes open we all retire to our rooms, and that's when I hear Jade on the phone with Cadence. I quietly tiptoe to Jade's room and put my ear to the door to see if I can hear what they are talking about. I can make out something about clothes, a party, and then I hear her say something about a tux. I don't have to wear a tux. What are they talking about? I hear Dad clear his throat behind me.

"What are you doing?" he asks and I turn to tell him to be quiet. He shakes his head and motions for me to follow him.

As we walk into the kitchen he tells me to take a seat.

"Why are you listening at your sister's door?"

"I don't know."

"Barrick. Answer the question."

"I overheard her on the phone with Cadence. I wanted to know if she was talking about me."

"Here we go," Dad says as he sits back and crosses his arms. "Spill it."

"I asked her to The Loft for New Year's. I knew Jade was going with Aaron, and didn't want her to be alone."

"Yeah, you keep tellin' yourself that, son," he says with a laugh.

"What's that supposed to mean?"

"You know that you wanted to ask her. Don't make it look like a pity date."

I don't say anything because he's right. "Dad, I overheard Jade say something about a tux. Do you think she has a boyfriend back home?"

"I have no clue, but that's something you're going to have to trust her on. You also have to remember that she's not from 'round here. She's from a different world, and you can't fit a square inside a circle," he says as he stands and leaves me at the table. "Oh, and don't do that to your sister. Would you want her doing that to you?" I shake my head no and call it a night.

34

CADENCE

I wake early to do my part on the farm before I leave, but I mostly want more time with Barrick this morning. I make sure to apply my makeup perfectly before going to the barn.

I notice that Barrick's early and has already gotten started when I walk into the barn. He looks up when he hears me and I'm unsure I like the look on his face.

"Are you okay?" I ask.

"Yeah, why?"

"No reason," I say as I start to help him.

As we work, he doesn't say much and it's obvious something is on his mind. When I can't take it anymore, I stop what I'm doing and walk over to him.

"Will you tell me what your problem is?" I say with my arms crossed.

"I'm fine," he says and everyone knows that fine doesn't mean fine. I stand there and stare at him. "What?" he questions.

"When I saw you yesterday you were normal Barrick, but today you look like you're mad at the world. What's going on?"

He continues to work and I continue to stand there. "I'm not moving until you talk to me."

"Won't you miss your flight?" he says with an attitude.

"What's that supposed to mean?"

"Nothin'," he says as he stands to walk toward the sink and I follow.

"Oh it means something. How can you go from asking me out to giving me the cold shoulder in less than twenty-four hours? What did I do?" I demand.

He takes a deep breath and turns to me. "I overheard Jade talking to you last night."

"Okay," I say and rack my brain for something that would have made him mad. I can't come up with anything. "So you were being nosey and you're mad at me? That doesn't make any sense."

"It doesn't matter," he says.

"Yes, it does. Just tell me what you thought you heard. I'm not leaving here until you tell me."

He looks me straight in the eye and asks, "Why was Jade talking about a tux? I don't need a tux for New Year's." Then it hits me. He overheard me talking about Lauren's plans for Jack Moore.

"Are you serious right now? For starters, you just asked me out on a real date twenty-four hours ago. How do you have any claim to me yet? Maybe I'll decide I don't like you that much." He looks hurt so I take a deep breath and start to explain. "I have to go to a party tomorrow night. It's super fancy. I was telling your sister about my friend, Lauren. She's got the hots for Jack Moore. His parents are throwing the party. She couldn't believe that people actually get that dressed up for a party. That's all."

He stands there as if he doesn't believe me. "Barrick, I don't know what's going through your mind right now, but I can assure you that I don't want anything to do with him. He's just like my dad. All of them are, and I don't want anyone that is anything like him," I say as I take a step forward and look into his eyes. "I promise," I say as I wrap my arms around his neck.

"Cadence!" I hear Mom yell as I jump out of Barrick's arms. "You about ready?" she questions.

"Yeah, just a minute. We're almost finished," I say as I look back at him. "I promise," I say and he smiles.

"You better go," he says.

I turn to walk out of the barn but glance back over my shoulder to find him watching me. I can't wait for New Year's Eve.

Walking to the house, I get my suitcase and when I return to the foyer Barrick is standing there. "Let me get that for you," he says with a smile. The four of us walk to the front porch. Barrick takes my suitcase to the Suburban while I tell Gran bye. I didn't think leaving her would be this difficult. Mom and I walk to the truck. Barrick is still standing there and I look at Mom, who gives me a nod. I tell him thank you and give him a kiss on the cheek goodbye. He gives me a smile and I tell him I'll see him in five days.

I can tell Mom is nervous as she drives me to the airport. She tries to act as if this isn't a big deal, but I know she's worried I won't want to come back.

"Mom it's going to be fine," I say as confidently as I can.

"I know. I just worry about you traveling alone."

"I'm a big girl," I say with a laugh.

"Don't remind me," she says.

When we get to the airport, Mom helps me get my suitcase then she hugs me tightly. I promise to call her once I'm through security and again when I land. I walk inside and see her pull away.

Once I'm through security I do as promised and call Mom and then text Lauren that I'm one step closer to seeing her. She sends me overly-excited emojis. Before long they are calling for passengers to board the plane. We're in the air and on the ground before I have time to finish my book.

As I power on my phone, I see a message from an unknown number letting me know they are here. I guess Bimbo has arrived. I tell her I'm on the ground and will be out soon, then text Mom and

Lauren. Placing my phone in my purse, I stand to grab my carry-on bag when I hear a new text message alert from a number I don't know.

Unknown: I stole your number from my sister. Hope you had a great flight.

I quickly save his number and then reply.

Me: Sneaky are we! I just landed.

Walking to the baggage claim, I look for the bimbo. I hear my phone again. It's her and of course she's waiting outside.

Rolling my eyes as well as my luggage, I walk outside to look for her. I spot her in a brand new SL Roadster. I'd bet my entire savings that my dad bought it. She doesn't bother to get out she just pops the trunk instead. I place my stuff in the trunk then slide into the passenger seat.

I quickly adjust my sunglasses so I don't have look at her directly. "How was your flight?" she asks.

"Good," I state.

"Great! I've got an awesome afternoon planned for us. We're going to get mani-pedis and then we're going shopping. Your dad has given me strict instructions to buy you whatever you want."

"You're joking?" I question.

"Not at all," she says as she floors it and we drive to an upscale salon. She walks in like she's important. "Reservation for Lewis." *What did she say?*

The cute girl that welcomed us tells us to follow her. We take a seat in massage chairs for our pedicures. "Mrs. Lewis, would you like a glass of wine?" I quickly turn my head and almost break my neck.

"Excuse me miss, but I'm Miss Lewis, not her," I say with attitude.

"Oh, I'm so sorry," she says and Bimbo gives me a nasty look. I can see she hasn't changed.

We are civil to each other from this point on, but we both know that this is just for appearance. We go our separate ways as soon as we get to the mall. I find a ton of clothes, but can't bring myself to buy most of them. There's no way I'll wear them in Delight. However, I can't resist a new designer gown for tonight and an outfit for New

Year's Eve. I text several pictures to Jade to see what she thinks. Of course she loves them, and jokingly tells me to bring her something back. I must have read her mind because I already picked out a designer necklace for her to go with one of those awful mono-grammed vests she wears.

I meet up with Bimbo and check out. She doesn't say much, but when we are almost to Dad's she gives me a speech about being nice and not giving my dad any trouble. *When have I ever been trouble?*

Dad is waiting for us by the front door with a glass of scotch in his hand. He sets it down and gives me a hug. He takes a step back and looks at me.

"You look beautiful, Cadence." He turns and looks at both of us. "We don't have long before the party. You might want to get ready."

"Of course," I say as I take my things to the guest bedroom.

Before I take a shower, I make a quick call to Lauren letting her know I made it through the afternoon with Bimbo and that I can't wait to see her.

I take my time getting ready. I want to look flawless for my dad. He expects nothing but the best. I slide into the new Halston Heritage cocktail dress, which fits perfectly. I love dressing up. I slide on the matching high heels and look in the mirror once more before leaving with Dad.

A valet stand is set up in front of the Moore's home and a valet assists me out of the car. Bimbo loops her arm around Dad and I do my best not to trip her. As we enter the main room, I look around for Lauren or some other teen that I know. Dad sees me scan the room and tells me to stay with him for now. We make our rounds and he introduces me to new faces, and when we've made our rounds he dismisses me like a servant.

Taking a glass of sparkling juice, I walk toward my group of friends. I take a big gulp when I see Jack Moore turn toward me. He gives me a wide grin and I smile back as I walk toward him.

"You look amazing, Cadence," he says.

"Not so bad yourself," I say. "Lauren!" I yell as I see her coming through the doorway. I run around Jack and hug her tightly.

"Was Jack talking to you?" she questions.

"Yeah, but he's all yours," I wink.

For the next three hours I talk with Lauren and all my other friends from my old school. They tell me the scoop on everyone and as the evening comes to an end, Dad approaches me to tell me it's time to leave. Lauren and I have already schemed for me to go to her house. It takes a little bit of effort, but he finally gives in. The only request is that I come home by noon tomorrow. No problem.

I tell him bye and leave with Lauren and her parents. As soon as we are at her apartment, we change clothes and have a full-out gab session on everything that has been going on. When we are no longer able to laugh, cry, or keep our eyes open, we fall asleep.

I wake up before it's daylight, and I can only assume it's Gran's fault. I toss and turn and then decide to check my social media. No one else is up and I don't want to wake them so I try to close my eyes. I doze off, but at eight thirty I'm up again and need to get up. I hear someone stirring. I quietly leave Lauren in the bed and make my way to the kitchen where I find her mom.

"You're up early," she says.

"I've been up before it was light."

"Did you not sleep well?" she asks with concern.

"Oh, no. Since I've been at Gran's, I've had to get up to work."

"Work?" she says with confusion.

"On the farm. It's nothing I enjoy but I have to if I want to stay on Gran's good side."

She gives me a slight smile and then pours me a cup of coffee. "Morning, sleepy head," I say to Lauren as she shuffles into the kitchen.

"When did you become a morning person?" she asks.

"Don't ask," I say with a laugh. "Are we going to the studio today?" I question.

"I thought you had to be back at noon." I shrug my shoulders as if I don't care.

We eat breakfast and I tell her mom about life at Gran's. Watching her expressions is like a horror movie, especially when I tell her about milking a cow by hand, but when I tell her about the monogramming she looks as if she'll die. Believe me, I feel her pain.

Lauren and I get dressed and I seriously want to go to the studio, but she insists that I do as Dad wishes. I take the subway to Dad's house and am angry that he's not home. I could have just stayed at Lauren's. I send him a text and walk to the studio.

Opening the double glass doors, I feel butterflies in my stomach. I'm so happy to be back. Several of my friends greet me and tell me how much they missed me as I walk back to Madame's office. She welcomes me with a hug and I fill her in on my life. She acts as if she's listening, but I can see that her mind is elsewhere.

After two hours on the floor, I make my way back to Dad's. I feel like an outsider because there is nothing that reminds me of our family except for one picture on his desk from my recital last year.

I shower and take a moment to see what Jade is up to. She quickly tells me that her brother looks like a lost puppy and that makes me laugh. She tells me that everyone at the studio has asked where I am, and that she's excited about going out for New Year's.

I text Lauren to see what she wants to do tomorrow. We come up with a plan and then she informs me that Jack Moore has been blowing her phone up. I'm so excited for her; it's like a dream come true. I take a moment and relax until I hear Dad come home.

While we eat dinner he asks about my plans for the remainder of my stay, and then we retreat to the living room. Dad asks if I want to watch a movie, and it feels like old times. I can't help but say yes.

"Can we watch *The Game Plan?*" He smiles and Bimbo looks confused.

"Isn't that a kid movie?" she questions.

"So?" I say to her. "Dad and I always watched it together. Didn't we?" I turn to him.

"We did, and I think that sounds like a great idea."

We get all comfy in our chairs and I notice Bimbo is actually paying attention. I'm so happy to have a few hours where I don't have to worry about life. I just get to enjoy a glimpse of what my life was like when Dad was always with me.

As the credits roll, I see that Bimbo has fallen asleep, but Dad is still wide-awake.

"Cadence, want to go get some coffee?" he asks.

"Sure," I say. Dad and I leave Bimbo in the chair, and walk down the street to the closest coffee shop. We order and take a seat while we wait.

"I'm glad you're here," he says.

"Me too. I miss it here," I say to him.

He gets quiet as they call our names to get our coffee.

"I'm sorry about how things have been. It's been difficult to figure out a balance."

"Are you serious?" He nods. "I thought you were going to apologize for screwing around on Mom," I say bluntly.

"Cadence! I thought we were past that."

I laugh at him. "Oh, I can see that you are, that's for sure, but no worries I'm sure Mom and I will get there. I also thought you might apologize to your only daughter for uprooting her, screwing up her future and forgetting to call her."

Standing, I no longer want to be here. Dad stands as well and we walk back to his apartment. The living room is empty when we walk in. Dad tries to apologize, but I don't want to hear it. He offers to take me shopping tomorrow. *He's joking right? He can't use money to fix this.* I hatefully tell him goodnight and go to my room.

I pick up my phone and call Mom. She answers with concern in her voice. I tell her that I want to come home now, but she refuses to let me. I get angrier by the minute. She tells me to calm down and to call her in the morning. She believes that if I sleep on it I will change my mind as she reminds me that I've wanted to be in New York since I've left. Taking a deep breath, I know she's right. I calm down and tell her I love her.

BARRICK

Cadence has barely been gone twenty-four hours and I'm going crazy. I can't forget the comment about not being official or whatever. Heck no we're not official, but I dare tuxedo boy to touch her. I'd go redneck quick. Unable to shake it, I decide to talk to Jade.

"Come in," she says as I knock on her door.

"You got a minute?" I ask her.

"Always for you," she says as I take a seat on her bed.

"What are you doing?" I ask her, knowing it's quite obvious.

"Painting my nails. Would you like me to do yours?" she asks, moving closer to me.

"Nah. Purple isn't my color."

"What's going on?"

"Do you think Cadence misses this place?"

"I have no idea. She's texted me a few times, but seems to be having fun."

"Did she mention anything about that party?" I ask, fishing for answers.

"Yeah, she said it was fancy. She hung out with her old friends and spent the night at Lauren's. Oh my gosh, she sent me a pic of the dress. Barrick, it was amazing." She grabs her phone and shows me. Holy moly. The way the red complements her hair is the second thing I notice. The dress is super short, and her legs go on for days. "Stop drooling, Romeo." She giggles.

"I'm not," I say, but she just gives me a look. "Did she mention anything else?"

Jade pauses and looks at me. "If you are wondering if there was a date or guy, the answer is no. Stop being such a worrywart before I paint that on your forehead," she says, holding the nail polish too close to me.

I run my fingers through my hair. This girl, who I haven't even been on a real date with yet, is driving me crazy. "You promise not to get mad if I tell you something?" I ask her.

"Yeah."

"I listened to you talking to her the other night before she left. I heard you talking about a tux. I asked her about it. Of course she got an attitude, but then told me I had nothing to worry about. Do you think she's telling the truth?"

"Okay, I can see that me being friends with your wannabe girl-friend is going to be tough. From what she told me and without breaking girl code, you have nothing to worry about. Now if you're done asking me twenty questions, I want to get back to painting my nails and watching *Party Down South.*

I can't believe she watches that crap. Leaving her room, I go to mine, and do my best to believe what my sister has said. The next ninety-six hours are going to feel like an eternity.

CADENCE

*T*he following morning I'm not surprised to find that I'm in the apartment alone. I grab a bite to eat and slide on my dance clothes before calling Lauren.

"Wake up, sleepyhead," I say to her as she groggily answers the phone.

"Why do you have to be so awake? It's only nine," she mumbles.

"What time are we going?" I ask her.

"Eleven."

"Okay, I'll see you there," I say as I disconnect. I really wanted to talk to her about what happened with Dad last night, but I can see that's out. What am I going to do for two hours? I watch TV and read before going to the subway.

As I walk the short distance, I look at the world around me. I notice that everyone here is in a hurry, people don't smile, and that they expect others to move out of the way. I've never noticed that before.

I'm not surprised when I beat Lauren to the studio. She arrives shortly after I do with a coffee in her hand, and I can tell she's barely awake.

"Girl, you better hurry up with that cup of joe. We've got dancin' to do," I say.

"You've got to stop being so excited this early. And did you just pull out a Southern twang? I'm seriously starting to worry about you." She laughs.

We take our places and it feels amazing to stretch and dance with her. When we take a break, she asks if I want to see our piece now that it's been modified into a solo. I feel uneasy, but agree.

Taking a seat on the wooden floor, I watch how the duet has been transformed to spotlight Lauren. It's amazing and she is as flawless as ever, but the dark and twisted side it once had has vanished. It's perfect for her but I'm sad that she didn't keep some of my part in it.

"What did you think?" she asks when it's over.

"I loved it for you, but I do miss the rawness it once had." She pauses and looks at me. "What?" I ask.

"Nothing. I can't believe you think I would have kept that part. That's totally you."

"I guess you're right. So when we finish, do you want to hang out? I'm not going back to Dad's until I have to."

"Of course! There's a huge sale at the mall. We should totally check it out, and I heard there's a party tonight."

"I'm game," I say. We dance for another hour before we go our separate ways to get changed. Lauren says she'll meet me at Dad's.

Bimbo is there when I get to the house and she's in a chipper mood, which crushes my good one. I ignore her and go get ready. I text Dad my plans and he tells me to take his credit card. *I think I will.*

Bimbo lets Lauren in the door and when she knocks on my bedroom door, her face says exactly what I'm feeling.

"What does he see in her?" she asks.

"No brain and a nice rack, I guess," I say, shrugging my shoulders as I finish putting on my mascara. Lauren walks to my bed and notices the dress I bought for New Year's.

"That's fancy," she says.

"Yeah it's for New Year's Eve. Do you like it?" I ask.

"Yeah, but aren't you flying out that morning?" she questions.

"Um hum," I say, focusing on the mirror.

"What aren't you telling me?" she questions and is now looking at me in the mirror.

"I'm going out. It's New Year's," I say like she should know that already.

"What? With who? Oh, please don't tell me you're hooking up with some redneck cowboy down there."

"I'm not hooking up with a redneck cowboy. I'm going on a date with Barrick. You know, the guy who works for my Gran."

"Oh yeah, you were supposed to send me a picture of him. Are you about ready? Just being near wannabe Barbie is driving me crazy. I can't imagine having to spend time with her." Lauren is right. I quickly grab my coat, purse and Dad's credit card as we walk to the door.

"Where are you two going?" Bimbo asks.

"Dad knows," I say without giving her time to respond or ask another question. I open the door and we walk to the elevator.

As we make our way to the subway, I realize I didn't bring anything for tonight.

"Oh no! I didn't even pack clothes for tonight."

"Guess that means you can use Daddy's money," Lauren states.

"Yeah, but I'd rather not."

"What's wrong with you? First you've got some secret party for New Year's and now you don't want to spend dear old Dad's money? The Cadence I know never thought twice about swiping Dad's plastic. Where is Cadence and what have you done with her?"

"Things are different. He can't expect to buy my love, Lauren. That's just wrong," I explain. Lauren doesn't say anything else but I know she wants to. I can guarantee that she will sooner or later.

We stop in all of our usual spots, but I see a section that has blinged-out denim and smile as I pause by the rack.

"What are you doing?" Lauren asks with her nose turned up.

"These are what everyone wears at Gran's. I've never seen them here. In fact, I don't even know the brand, it just looks like an 'M' on your rear." *Miss Me.* "You want to try a pair on just for fun?" I ask.

"No! Please tell me those hillbillies aren't rubbing off on you," she states and I laugh, but I realize I kind of want to try them on. *What is wrong with me?* I dismiss the thought when Lauren eyes a new Michael Kors purse, and it is to die for. The sales clerk lets us look at it and I would love to have it.

"You know you want it, Cadence."

"Yeah I do, but I don't want to spend my dad's money," I say flatly.

"What is wrong with you? You have a credit card with no limits, and you're debating this? If I were you, I'd forget what he did and spend all of his money." I'm appalled by her comment.

"You can't be serious? He messed around on my mom, made me move to the middle of nowhere, and you think that a purse and a new designer outfit can fix it? I think not."

"I think you're wrong," she says, taking the purse and telling the cashier we'll take it. In this moment, I've realized that Lauren and I may be more different than I ever imagined. I take out my card and swipe it before telling Lauren *Merry Christmas.*

"So who's having a party tonight?" I ask as we're sitting on the subway scrolling through social media.

"Does it matter? It's a party!" she states as she grabs my phone. "So is that one of the losers you're dancing with now?"

"She's not a loser. It's Jade," I state trying to hide the anger in my voice. I mean, I know I've said some ugly things to Lauren about everyone else in Delight, but I'm allowed. I'm the one that has to live there, but Jade is the most caring person I know.

"Sorry," she states, scrolling down the feed. "Who is that?" she questions and I know without looking it's Barrick.

"That's Barrick," I say trying to act like it's no big deal. Looking at the date and time, I know that it was just taken. It's obvious he's been at Gran's, and that smile is perfect.

"He *is* cute, but he looks like he's been rolling around in dirt. Please tell me you don't find that attractive. That he's just a date to your little New Year's party. I could never see you with a guy like that. You're more of a businessman kind of girl. Oh, what if you tried to make him like the guys here? You know, like one of those crazy movies."

"There's no way I could change him. He's pretty set in his ways, not to mention how he looks fabulous in those jeans." I giggle.

Lauren pauses and stares at me. "I can't believe you even said that. You are so much better than him. I bet he doesn't even know how to tie a tie." She laughs and it pisses me off. *Have I really been this judgmental before?*

"Just give me my phone." I don't say another word the rest of the way back to her apartment.

Once we're dressed for the party, I take a look at us in the mirror. We both look polished and sophisticated. We're two girls ready to take on the night, but I feel like something is missing. I realize that I'm missing the people who actually care about me the most.

"You ready?" Lauren asks.

"Sure," I say with a smile.

The party is just a typical party with people drinking and acting stupid. Lauren and I have never been drinkers because of our dance regimen. We don't have time to recover from a hangover or the time to work twice as hard to keep from putting on a few extra pounds. Needless to say, watching everyone around us is comical. These people think they have it all together, but as I look around I see miniature versions of their parents. They think that this world is only about what you have, and making yourself number one.

I have no idea what has come over me since I've been home, but I'm more aware of people's behavior, and most importantly Lauren's. Everything I've watched her do has a purpose to make herself look good. I still can't believe she thought spending Dad's money would make me feel better.

My phone buzzes in my purse and I take it out to look at it. Jade sent me a text picture. I crinkle my nose when I look at it. They are obviously having a wild night in Delight. Barrick and a few other guys are covered in mud and smiling from ear to ear. It makes me smile.

"What's making you smile like that?" Lauren asks, and I show her.

"That's God-awful. That gives a new meaning to mud facial." She laughs.

"Lauren, get over yourself. Can't you see how much fun they are having?"

"They might be, but we wouldn't," she states.

"How do you know that?" I ask her.

"You're joking right?" I stare at her.

"I have no idea if it's fun or not, but since I've gotten back I've realized how fake everyone is around here." She gasps. "The Moore's look like they have money, but I overheard my dad talking and they are about to file for bankruptcy, my dad cheated on my mom and acts as if he and Bimbo are a perfect little family without me, and you of all people should know how bad that hurt me. Instead, you think making fun of my new friends and spending my dad's money is going to make me happy. It doesn't."

"Well, tell me what you really think, Cadence."

"Lauren, you've been my best friend since I can remember, but everyone is human and we all like different things, and we need to be respectful of that," I say to her.

"Cadence, I don't know what has happened to you. You used to be someone I understood, but this girl standing in front of me is a complete stranger." I couldn't agree more looking at her.

Lauren and I are relatively quiet the rest of the night, and I really want to go home... like to my mom, home.

BARRICK

When Aaron called to ask Jade and I to go mudding, we couldn't resist. We loaded up the four wheelers and took them down by the river, and by midnight we were all covered in mud and laughing. I saw Jade snap a picture and I hope she sent it to Cadence. I want to call or text her, but I don't want to smother her. Jade slides her phone back in her pocket and we load up the trailer and drive back to the house.

We take showers as soon as we get home and then she comes into my room.

"So I've got a question for ya, bro." I look at her and wait. "Are you planning something special for Cadence or is it just like any other New Year's at The Loft?"

"I was planning on it being a normal one. Jade, it's our first date. It's not like I'm proposing or something," I say, shaking my head.

"Well, are you getting her from the airport?" she asks.

"Her mom is doing that. Why all these questions?" I'm so confused right now.

"I thought I mentioned us picking her up. Maybe even Aaron could ride and we could grab something to eat in Charlotte before coming back here to get ready."

"Don't you have practice?" I ask her because she is always at the studio.

"No."

"I don't want to overstep where I'm not welcome."

Jade starts to laugh. "Oh, you're welcome all right." I have no idea what she's talking about. That girl is too much.

Lying on my bed, I take out my phone and debate calling or texting Cadence. I hate to wake her or bother her. Screw it. I do it anyway.

Me: Is it New Year's Eve yet?

Cadence: I wish!

Something about that comment makes me think things aren't going too great for her.

Me: How's it going?

Cadence: Okay

Me: Just okay?

She doesn't respond so I hit send on my phone and she picks up on the third ring. I can hear music and a lot of noise in the background.

"Hey, everything okay?" I ask her.

"I'm at a party with Lauren." She doesn't sound happy.

"Cadence, what's going on?"

"Nothing," she says and it's obvious that something is bothering her, but I also know not to push it.

"Okay, well, I guess I'll just see you Friday." I'm worried about her.

Just as I'm about to hang up I hear, "Hey Barrick, can you call me tomorrow? I'm not somewhere I can talk."

"Absolutely." I hang up and wish I could be there with her.

CADENCE

I go home with Lauren after the party but we still don't say much. The tension between us is ridiculous. I think about going to Dad's, but veto the idea when I look at the time. I'm not taking the subway alone at this time of night.

Lying in bed, my mind begins to work overtime. It's like it's on repeat of Lauren being a greedy spoiled brat, her bad mouthing Jade and Barrick, and then Barrick calling tonight. I feel like I'm pulled between two different worlds. I toss and turn until my mind finally gives in and I drift off to sleep.

When the sun peers through the window, I'm wide-awake and of course Lauren is still snoozing. I get out of bed, shower, and get ready. As I walk out of the bathroom, she asks me what I'm doing.

"I think I'm going to go home," I say to her and she looks at me like I'm crazy.

"Look I don't know what your deal was last night, but we've never argued and you moped around there like you hated every minute of it. You used to love parties. You have one more day before you fly out, don't waste it being mad at me." She's right. I'm not mad anymore. I'm over it.

"I'm not mad at you. I'm just going to Dad's. I probably should visit before I leave, and I've got a few things to do."

"Whatever," she says as she falls back in bed and in that moment I realize exactly what Barrick meant by how unattractive that word truly is.

"So you want to go to the bakery for breakfast before I go?" I ask and she shakes her head no. "Okay, well I guess I'm going to go."

"You're seriously leaving?" she asks me, slowly sitting up.

"Yeah. I've got a few things to do before I leave tomorrow. You want to hang out later?" I ask her.

"I can't. I've got practice, and a date with Jack."

"Oh, okay. Call me later," I say as I take my shopping bags and walk toward the subway. I'm almost positive she's not going to call.

On the way I decide to stop at the bakery anyway and order a croissant and coffee. The croissant melts in my mouth and I can't resist sending Barrick a picture of the flakey goodness. Within seconds my phone rings.

"So you're saving me a bite, right?" he questions without a hello.

"Doubtful." I laugh. "Aren't you supposed to be working?" I ask him.

"Yeah, but I think Ms. Mae would be okay with me taking a break for you." My heart flutters.

"Yeah right. You know she'd get all over you," I say.

"It would be worth it. Since it's now tomorrow, do you want to tell me what's really going on?" he asks.

"Let's just say that coming home hasn't been as much fun as I expected. Oh, guess what. They sell those jeans Jade wears at our mall," I state.

"Surely not," he says and I can feel his smile. "Jade and I were talking. How would you like for us to pick you up tomorrow?"

I want to say yes, but know that Mom and I need to talk. "I don't want you to have to do that," I say.

"It's not that big of a deal. Plus, I think Jade has this crazy plan she's wanting to put in action."

"I'll check with Mom and get back to you. I know she'll want to know about everything that happened."

"That's perfectly fine. Well, I better get back to work."

We disconnect and I take a moment to finish eating before going back to Dad's. I'm caught off guard when I see that he's at home.

"Everything okay?" I ask.

"Actually, yes. We need to talk." Oh Lord. He's about to start when Bimbo walks into the room. "Mindy, can you give us a minute." She smirks and walks back out of the room "I've got a job offer in Sweden. Mindy and I are going to be moving there at the first of the year." He states it like it's going to affect me.

"Okay," I respond, staring at him.

"You're not upset?" he questions, almost looking hurt.

I shrug my shoulders. "Dad, this is the first time I've seen you since I left four months ago. You've barely spent any time with me since I've been here, and it's obvious the two of you want to be one little happy family without a reminder of your past. I'm fine," I say but my hands begin to shake as the anger rises in my veins. I clasp them together because I refuse to let it show. "You're my dad and I love you," I say with a fake smile.

"It's not like that at all!" he yells. "I have given you everything you've wanted and made sure you had the best of the best. I don't know why trying to further my career is such an issue," he states.

"Nothing is wrong with furthering your career but what happened to the dad who would come and pick me up from the studio, who would let me paint his fingernails, and call me his favorite girl? I haven't seen him in a long time, and I miss him." My emotions take over and I start to cry.

Dad doesn't know what to say, and I don't want to discuss it anymore. "I'm going out," I say as I grab my purse and head for the mall. It's time for a little retail therapy.

When I get to the mall, I bypass all stores that would normally make me stop and look. I'm on a mission. If I'm going to spend my dad's money, it's going to be for some awesome gifts for others.

My first stop is the Miss Me section. I quickly text Jade to see what size she and Barrick wear. I grab two or three pairs without looking at the price then I find a top that is like nothing she would be able to find in North Carolina. After paying, I continue to walk through the mall. I've seen things that I like, but nothing that strikes me as Barrick's style.

I shop until I can't shop anymore. My arms are loaded down and I'm physically exhausted as I walk into Dad's apartment. I'm surprised when I hear Dad's voice.

"Cadence, we need to finish our talk."

"Fine, I'll be right back," I say as I walk to my room to put my bags down. Taking a deep breath I walk back to him. "Yes?"

"I've thought about what you've said, and I want you to know that I'm sorry you feel that way. I never meant to hurt you, but sometimes life has a different path for each of us." *Is he trying to say that he can't help it?*

"Did you really just tell me that things change and life moves on?" I am appalled that he has no regard for my feelings.

"Cadence, why do you have to be so difficult?"

"Me? Why do you have to be so selfish?"

"That's enough, young lady!" he says and I don't listen to another word as I storm off to my room, and pack my things. Forget this. I'm not staying here any longer.

As I begin to roll my things into the entranceway, Bimbo stops me. "I can't believe you're doing this to him," she smarts.

"Oh please! You're so ready for me to get out of here so you can live your wannabe Barbie life. I hope you two enjoy Sweden," I say like a smartass.

"Oh, you mean the three of us," she states. *Excuse me.*

"I'm not going with you," I seethe.

"I know," she says as she touches her stomach. *That can't be. There's no way. Please no.* She smiles and I want to scream as Dad appears.

"She's lying. Please tell me she's lying," I plead with my dad as he shakes his head. "I hate you!" As I start to walk out the door, he grabs my arms and pleads for me to stay. There's no way I'm staying here tonight. I grab a taxi for the airport, and as soon as I walk into the airport I use his credit card to switch my flight for one that leaves tonight.

BARRICK

I worked like crazy today on the farm trying to get ahead for tomorrow. I want to spend as much time with Cadence as possible when she gets home. I want to make this date a night to remember. Before leaving, I check on Daisy. She seems to be doing well, and in a few months a new calf will be here. Stopping by the house, I ask Regina if I need to pick Cadence up tomorrow, and she says that she would like to. I can't blame her.

Getting in my truck, I turn the ignition and make my way home. As I kill the engine my phone begins to ring, and I see Cadence's name.

"Hey!" I say with excitement, but that quickly fades when I hear her voice.

"I need you to come and get me," she says and I can tell she's trying to hold back tears.

"Where are you?" I question.

"I'm at the airport."

"In Charlotte?"

"No. My flight is boarding now. It will land in less than two hours."

"Are you okay?"

"I will be. Please just promise you'll be there."

"Of course."

We hang up and I have no idea what to do. Do I call her mom and Ms. Mae? Do I take Jade with me? I look at my clock and realize I've got about twenty minutes to decide before I need to get on the road. Jade isn't home, but my parents are. I walk in and briefly tell them what is going on and they suggest I call Ms. Mae and Regina.

"Hello?"

"Ms. Mae, it's Barrick."

"Is everything okay?" she questions.

"I'm not sure. Cadence just called and said she's boarding a plane to come home tonight. She wants me to pick her up, but there's something wrong with her."

"Regina!" she yells away from the phone. "Barrick is on the phone. Did you know Cadence is coming home?"

I hear the shuffle of the phone as Regina takes it. "Barrick, what do you mean she's on her way home?"

"She called a few minutes ago and was upset. She said she would be okay, and asked if I'd pick her up. I'm on my way now."

"I'm not sure what's going on, but I'll find out. Please text me and let me know when she's landed and that she is physically okay."

"Yes, ma'am," I say as I hang up and quickly call Jade. She's a mess and begging me to turn around and wait for her. There's no way. I won't risk not being there when she lands.

I put my truck in the wind and I make it to the airport with time to kill. I hurry to the baggage claim and scan the crowd. I don't see her. I glance at my phone for the time. I check the arrival board and scan for any flight coming from New Jersey or New York within the next fifteen minutes. *Bingo!* I hurry to baggage claim four and wait for what feels like an eternity. When I can't stand still any longer, I walk toward the escalator and look for her. *Nothing.* Finally, I see her descend but I don't see my little spitfire, I see a hollow shell. Even with a designer outfit, makeup, and all the superficial stuff, I can see that something is terribly wrong.

Stepping off the escalator she looks at me and I can see tears start to form. *Why does she have to cry on me?* She quickly pushes them back as we walk in silence to get her luggage. I don't say anything because frankly I'm not sure if she will cuss me out or cry. When her suitcase arrives, I grab it and walk her to my truck.

"Where to?" I ask.

"Anywhere but Gran's," she says as I quickly text Jade to let her know she's okay and for her to call Regina.

"You need to call your mom," I say quietly.

"Fine," she says, taking her phone from her purse.

I glance at her and see that she's trying so hard to be strong, but I think she's about to crumble.

"Here," she says bluntly, handing me the phone.

"Yes, ma'am," I say to Regina.

"It's her father. Give her some time and bring her home. For you to be the one she called, says a lot. Get my baby home safe."

"Yes, ma'am," I say as I hang up and hand Cadence her phone. She doesn't say anything, but as she leans her head against the glass I want to have her in my arms. I flip up the console, and tell her to come here. Without a word, she slides next to me and quietly wipes away the silent tears.

Arriving back in Delight, I only have a few places I can take her. Deciding that she's probably better off in the middle of nowhere, I turn onto a dirt road and pull into a field near a set of pine trees. She lifts her head from my shoulder to look around.

"You said you didn't want to go to Ms. Mae's."

"Thanks."

We sit in silence and I run my fingers through her hair to let her know it's okay.

"Can you tell me what's goin' on?" I finally ask. She pulls away from my chest and I brace myself for a good tongue-lashing from her.

"Let's just say that my visit didn't go as I had hoped."

"Okay, but why did you decide to leave without telling anyone?"

"I got in an argument with my dad."

"Why didn't you go to Lauren's?"

I see her breathing increase. "That wouldn't have worked out," she says as her eyes fill with tears as she continues. "I'm sorry. I shouldn't have called you. I'm so stupid."

"No, I'm glad you called, and I'm sorry if I'm asking too many questions. I can see that you are hurting so just talk to me. Please," I practically beg.

She doesn't say anything for a few minutes, but pulls her legs into her chest. "I thought going home would be easy. Barrick, they are all selfish," she says, looking me in the eyes. "You know what's worse?" I don't say anything, I just wait for her response. "My dad is the biggest one yet. I hate him." Tears begin to stream down her face. "I don't want to cry. I want to forget I even went." I have no idea what happened with her father or Lauren for that matter, but whatever it was has completely broken her. I take her in my arms, pull her onto my lap, and hold her while she cries on my shoulder.

When she seems to have stopped, I turn her chin toward me. "Cadence, whatever happened up there you can get beyond it. I promise I'll help you. You can depend on me." I want her to know I'll do anything to make her happy and feel loved.

"Thank you, Barrick. Can you take me home now?"

She just called her Gran's house home. I really like the sound of that.

To be continued...
Want a glimpse into Tutus & Cowboy Boots Part 2? Click here.

ABOUT THE AUTHOR

Casey Peeler grew up in North Carolina and still lives there with her husband and daughter.

Growing up Casey wasn't an avid reader or writer, but after reading Their Eyes Were Watching God by Zora Neal Hurston during her senior year of high school, and multiple Nicholas Sparks' novels, she found a hidden love and appreciation for reading. That love ignited the passion for writing several years later, and her writing style combines real life scenarios with morals and values teenagers need in their daily lives.

When Casey isn't writing, you can find her near a body of water listening to country music with a cold beverage and a great book.

Connect with Casey
http://www.authorcaseypeeler.com

CPSIA information can be obtained
at www.ICGtesting.com
Printed in the USA
LVHW010917190621
690647LV00012B/1083